THE MADNESS OF HUSBANDS

A Have Body, Will Guard Adventure Romance

by Neil S. Plakcy

Copyright 2016, 2020 Neil S. Plakcy. All rights reserved, including the right of reproduction in whole or in part in any form.

This book is a work of fiction. Names, characters, places, and incidents either are products of the author's imagination or are used fictitiously. Any resemblance to actual events or locales or persons, living or dead, is entirely coincidental.

Reviews for Neil Plakcy and the Have Body series:

"Never slows down" – Literary Nymphs Reviews on *Three Wrong Turns in the Desert*

"Plakcy's characters... charm" – Kirkus Reviews

"An engrossing writer" - Publisher's Weekly.

1 – The Angels' Share

After the clerk at the wine store disappeared into the back, Aidan Greene turned to Liam McCullough, who was browsing through the remainder boxes on the stone floor. "I called you my husband for the first time."

Liam, whom he had married only a few weeks before, looked up with a smile. "And?"

"It's such a simple word, and so much easier to use than all the synonyms, particularly in French," Aidan continued. "You can be *mon mari* instead of *mon partenaire domestique, mon compagnon, homme de ma vie, amour de ma vie…*"

"I hope I am still the love of your life," Liam said, still smiling. "Whether or not I put a ring on it."

"Who'd have thought, twenty years ago, when you were still a big, tough Navy SEAL, that one day you'd be married to a man and quoting Beyoncé?"

"Twenty years ago, there was no same-sex marriage and Beyoncé was a member of a girl group trying to get a guy to say her name while screwing."

"I never have that problem." Aidan half-closed his eyes, opened his mouth, and languorously said, "Lee-ammm."

Liam laughed. "You are still such a goof." He leaned back down to the remainder boxes, his sleeveless T-shirt tight to his waist, accenting his rippling biceps. His gold nipple rings pressed against the fabric.

When you lived with someone for so long, Aidan thought, it was easy to forget how handsome he was. Liam's square jaw and deep-set green eyes, combined with his impressive physique, reminded Aidan of action-adventure movie stars.

Aidan considered himself much more ordinary, though he'd had his share of admirers who were attracted by his brown eyes, his easy smile, and his shaggy brown hair, now tamed in a much shorter cut. Since joining Liam in close protection work, he had developed biceps of his own, though nowhere as impressive as Liam's, and he'd kept his waist narrow.

The wedding had drained their collection of wine as they served and toasted with their guests, so a friend had recommended a wine shop called *La Part des Anges* in Vieux Nice. "The name refers to the alcohol that evaporates through a barrel during the wine fermentation process," the friend had said. "They call it the angels' share."

The store was lined with shelves of wine bottles, and the floor was filled with wicker baskets of spices, boxes of glasses, corkscrews and other equipment. It was dim and smelled slightly musty, the residue of thousands of tastings hanging in the air.

Aidan and Liam had tasted the output of ten different vineyards, choosing to buy two cases of assorted bottles. Aidan felt a little dizzy from all the wine and was glad that Liam had driven them down into the old city from their home in Banneret-les-Vaux, where they had a small house and yard in the foothills of the Alpes-Maritimes.

They had taken time off to prepare for the wedding, and then had decided not to take a honeymoon—they had already traveled to many places in the course of their work in close protection, from Tunisia, where they met, to the United States to Corsica to Turkey, and most recently to Russia and Chechnya. They chose a staycation instead—taking a series of three-day weekends to relax and enjoy the places on the Côte d'Azur they had never visited or had begun to take for granted.

"Here is your wine," the clerk said, stacking the second box on the counter. "You have a car nearby?"

"In the garage a few blocks away," Liam said. "We can carry it."

Right, Aidan grumbled to himself. Liam was as sturdy and strong as he'd been as a SEAL, though the intervening ten years had turned a few strands of his dirty-blond hair white, and he couldn't do as many pushups or sit-ups as he once had. Aidan had never been as muscular, though he exercised with Liam nearly every day to maintain his flexibility.

Liam lifted one of the boxes of bottles to his shoulder, then put it back down on the counter. "Maybe we will borrow a hand truck from you," he said.

Aidan was surprised but said nothing. Liam was in his early forties by then, and they had both become more careful about doing anything that might hurt their bodies. They were no longer active bodyguards, but they maintained a relationship with the company that had employed them, Agence de Securité, and still took on the occasional job to keep their hands in.

It was a hot day, and the sun was directly overhead so there was little shade on the narrow cobblestone streets. Liam grumbled every time the hand truck's wheel stuck or jumped over a rock, and a fine sheen of sweat formed on his forehead.

By the time they reached the garage where they had left the Jeep, Aidan was dripping with sweat. It ran down the side of his head, dripped into his eyes, and pooled under his arms. *It must be global warming,* he thought, as he lifted each case of wine and stowed it in the back of the Jeep. They had been in Nice for nearly seven years, and January had never been so hot.

They rarely used air conditioning in the Jeep, preferring to leave the flaps up especially during the temperate winters. But when Liam started the Jeep, as if he read Aidan's mind, he turned the air conditioning on full blast.

They circled around a series of one-way streets to return to the store. Liam waited in a no-parking zone while Aidan hurriedly gave back the hand truck, and as Aidan got back to the Jeep he saw his husband leaning down, his face in front of the vent, letting the cold air push over him.

"Where to now?" Liam asked, when Aidan got back in.

The wine shop was only one item on their staycation list. They had shopped at the open-air market at the *Cours Saleya*, with its riot of fresh flowers and produce, the air a mix of fresh fish and fragrant herbs. They had bought olive oil from a local manufacturer and had eaten at five-star restaurants that had been on their wish list for years, as well as at local delights they discovered while venturing to unfamiliar neighborhoods.

Liam had begun to study at a Vietnamese martial arts studio in Nice, and Aidan had embarked on a pastry-making course at a patisserie famous for its macarons and chocolate cakes. He had taken a dozen different cooking courses in the past, when he lived with his previous boyfriend, Blake, in Philadelphia, and he had missed the chance to learn new skills.

"Head toward Saint-Jean-Cap-Ferrat," Aidan said. "We're going to the Paloma Beach Club for a swim and lunch."

"Private club?" Liam asked. "How'd you get access?"

"Probably the only place there that isn't private," Aidan said. "Named after Picasso's daughter because he and his family used to swim there. The beach is sheltered, and the restaurant is excellent, or at least so I read."

They took the Quai des États Unis around the bulk of Mont Boron, below the spot where Liam had proposed at the ruins that provided a panoramic view of the Bay of Angels and the old town. As they passed the port, Aidan noticed a giant American cruise ship was docked across from them, next to the breakwater. His cousin Ellen and her family had come to the wedding, and then taken a Mediterranean cruise on that same ship.

It had been wonderful to see her, her husband and kids, a bittersweet reminder of how they had been close growing up, and then when Aidan lived in Philadelphia, only an hour's drive from Ellen's home in North Jersey. He sighed. Maybe they'd get back to the States in a couple of years.

A long trip along the Boulevard Carnot took them through the part of Nice that tourists rarely saw, past offices and real estate agencies and a huge Carrefour supermarket. The *notaire* who had handled the sale of their home was out there. Aidan remembered how nervous he had been as he and Liam signed the papers for the small house in Banneret. What it had meant to him then to know that he and Liam were settling down, buying property together. At the time same-sex marriage was still illegal in France and in the US, and they'd both considered that joint purchase a celebration of their relationship. For years after, they'd joked that Notaire Justeau was the one who had committed them to each other.

"Remember Notaire Justeau?" Aidan asked, as they passed the office.

"How could I forget?" Liam said. "Those big brown eyes, that happy smile. The way he licked my hand."

"You're thinking of his dog," Aidan said, elbowing him. In truth, the notaire had been a young man, barely finished with his master's in law, and excited that Aidan and Liam had been the first same-sex couple whose papers he had processed.

They had so much history in Nice already, Aidan thought, as they rounded the Pointe Sans Culottes. The Mediterranean appeared to their right, waves crashing against the rocky shore. The wedding had reinforced that to him – he had surprised himself with the number of friends they had made in Nice and its environs, and the crowd had threatened to overflow the chairs they'd set up in the backyard.

Every place they passed seemed to stir a memory for Aidan. They rode high above the bay of Villefranche, and Aidan said, "Remember that family we worked for down there?"

"The Canadians, eh?" Liam said, mimicking their accent. It was one of their easier jobs – the husband was an oil billionaire from Alberta, paranoid about someone trying to sabotage his family's vacation, and they had spent ten days in a luxurious home overlooking the peninsula of Saint-Jean-Cap-Ferrat. They had swum in the private pool, eaten at excellent restaurants, and spent most of the time reassuring their client that he and his family were in no danger.

It was typical of the assignments they had taken on during their years with the Agence. Clients with fears who needed more reassurance than protection. Not that there hadn't been dangerous assignments—there had been. But it was much more pleasant to remember the easy jobs than the hard ones.

They drove past Saint-Jean-Cap-Ferrat's port, a sprawl of small boats rocking on gentle waves. "We're early for our lunch reservation," Aidan said. "Let's stop and take a walk."

"You're the boss," Liam said, as he parked near the waterfront.

They strolled past sea-themed artwork like a three-foot wide bronze crab and a planter shaped like a giant conch, with bright pink bougainvillea spilling out of it. "I'm glad we decided to do this staycation thing, though at first I was sure it was an excuse to lay around and do nothing," Liam said. "There are so many beautiful parts to this area that we never get to see."

"You obviously were ignoring my impressive organizational skills," Aidan said.

"I've learned never to underestimate you," Liam said.

"And when was the first time you recognized that?"

Liam cocked his head in thought. "I think the first time I realized you had hidden depths was when those men attacked us in the medina in Tunis," he said after a moment. "And you went right for that guy's balls, and squeezed, and then disappeared."

"I learned to fight dirty when I was a teenager and a guy tried to bully me," Aidan said. "Grabbing him down there scared the shit out of him. After that guys still called me names, but nobody got close to me."

"And when where you first impressed with me?" Liam asked.

"That's easy. The very first time I saw you, showering naked behind the Bar Mamounia." He grinned at his husband. "How could I not be impressed by that handsome face, those muscles, and your dick of death."

"You are still such a horndog, after all these years." Liam leaned down and placed a quick peck behind Aidan's ear. "And I still love it," he whispered.

They circled back to the car for the short hop to Club Paloma, set on a gorgeous round beach circled by high rock formations. They secured a pair of chaise-longues, then changed into their bathing suits. Aidan had long since adapted the European custom of wearing tiny bikinis, proud of the way they hugged his high, tight ass and fit snugly over his three-piece set.

Liam, despite his general tendency toward exhibitionism, favored board shorts in somber colors. Aidan didn't mind; he knew he'd be seeing what was under them later that evening.

They walked down the sandy shore, rare along the Cote d'Azur where many beaches were pebbled, and then dunked into the water. Liam immediately took off in the combat stroke he had learned as a SEAL. It was a combination of the breaststroke and freestyle that reduced resistance on a swimmer's body and made him harder to spot underwater.

Aidan leisurely swam overhand out into the bay, then turned back, doing five ocean laps. Then he climbed out of the water, shook himself like their little dog Hayam did, and dried off. He ordered a platter of fresh seafood and a pair of cocktails of Citron vodka and fresh-squeezed grapefruit juice, and it all arrived as Liam pulled himself out of the bay.

The view of the resort of Beaulieu and the cliffs of the Cap d'Ail was spellbinding, but Aidan only had eyes for his husband and the way the droplets of water cascaded over his square pecs, each nipple pierced with a simple gold ring. The thought of what he'd do with those nipples later made Aidan hard, and he bunched his towel over his abdomen.

It wasn't just that the rest of Liam's body was gorgeous, too—bulging biceps, narrow waist, muscled calves and thighs. It was the connection they had built over the nearly nine years they had been together. Liam's intelligence, his ability to react well in danger, the sense Aidan had of being protected in his arms.

Maybe there were men out there who had different tastes, who wouldn't find Liam as appealing as Aidan did, but that's because they didn't know him.

"Get your tongue back in your mouth," Liam teased as he walked up to their chairs. He grabbed a towel and dried his hair, and Aidan's mouth went dry at the sight of those arms flexing. Then Liam tied the towel around his waist and sat on the other chair.

He raised a cocktail to Aidan's in a toast, and Aidan said, "To my handsome husband."

Liam clinked his glass and said, "Over the teeth and past the gums, look out stomach, here it comes."

Aidan started to laugh. "You know how to ruin a romantic moment."

"There will be plenty of those when we get back to the house, won't there?"

"There certainly will be. For now, I want to relax and enjoy the view."

"I can tell you're enjoying it by the way you're covering up your dick."

"Drink your cocktail, sailor." Aidan pulled out his phone and began to take pictures of the yachts and sailboats in the harbor, the panorama around him, and the clifftop town of Èze, surrounded by banana and orange trees and lush green date palms.

He checked in on Facebook, uploading a couple of the photos for his family back in the States and his friends in Nice. Then he looked up at the top of the screen, and the little squiggle in the circle indicated he had a new message. He clicked on it and was stunned to see it was from Blake Chennault, the man he'd spent eleven years with back in Philadelphia.

"Holy shit." He had accepted a friend request from Blake a few years before, but Blake never posted and they'd had no real contact since Blake had tracked him down to Liam's small house behind the Bar Mamounia in Tunis and pleaded with him to come back.

And now Blake wanted something else. "I need your help, and this is the only way I have to contact you," Blake wrote. "Please call me as soon as possible. It's a matter of life and death." He had added a phone number with a Philadelphia area code.

As if Aidan didn't know that number by heart, even after all this time. It had been his number for eleven years, after all. Some things did not change.

"What's so exciting on your phone?" Liam asked.

"Blake Chennault," he said, showing the phone to Liam. "A matter of life and death."

"Then you'd better call him," Liam said, and though Aidan listened there wasn't any jealousy in his voice. "There's a path along the water, and I'm going to get in a run. You can fill me in when I get back."

Liam slid on his sneakers and socks, and after a couple of quick stretches, took off at a slow jog.

Aidan stared at the phone in his hand. Had it really been eight and a half years since the day Blake had kicked him to the curb, back in Philadelphia? So much had happened—falling in love with Liam, adventures together, continents spanned, intimate embraces.

How had that time evaporated, sneaking away like the angels' share of those bottles they had sampled that morning?

2 – Trust

Aidan checked the time before he called Philadelphia. It was six hours earlier there, which made it about noon on Friday. Why would Blake be at home on a workday? Blake never took days off. At least, he hadn't when Aidan had known him.

He called the number, and Blake picked up almost immediately. "Hello, Blake. It's Aidan."

It felt strange to hear Blake's voice on the phone again, as if they'd spoken only the day before. "Thank God I reached you." There was a desperation in Blake's voice Aidan had never heard. "I need to hire bodyguards for Ricardo starting next week."

Aidan looked out at the sea, where a giant white pelican swooped down to the water, then rose up again with a fish wriggling in its beak. "Slow down, Blake. It's been nearly nine years since the last time we talked. Who is Ricardo?"

"My husband. He's a diplomat from Argentina, working for a think tank here in Philadelphia." He sighed. "It's a long story, but I'll give you the quick picture. In October he had a psychotic break and had to be hospitalized. He's still heavily medicated, and part of his problem is paranoia. He's frightened of everything."

"We're not psychiatrists, Blake," Aidan said, trying for gentleness in his voice.

"Believe me, he has enough of them. He doesn't sleep at night – he only naps during the day, and only when I'm home to watch over him.

He won't go out after dark, which means we can't go out to dinner or to meet with friends."

Aidan listened. This was the worst kind of close protection assignment, when the threat was all in the client's head. He and Liam had taken on that kind of job once, for a wealthy Niçoise businessman. It dragged on for two weeks until finally the man's family had him hospitalized.

"About six months ago, Ricardo accepted an opportunity to speak at a conference in Nassau next week," Blake continued. "The topic is *The Position of Jews in Latin and South America*, so of course Ricardo accepted."

"Why of course?"

"His last name is Levy," Blake said. "Of course he's Jewish. Don't you keep up?"

"Keep up with what, exactly?" Aidan asked. "Honestly, Blake, I haven't thought a whole lot about you since I saw you in Tunis."

"But you accepted my friend request on Facebook."

"I did. But it's not like I've been stalking you. I can't even remember the last thing you posted."

"We're getting off track here," Blake said. "The conference is from January 21st to the 24th. Ricardo would like you to meet us here in Philadelphia on the 20th and fly to Nassau with us. I'll cover all your travel expenses and whatever your daily rate is, and I've already reserved a two-bedroom suite at the Atlantis for the four of us."

"Hold on, Blake. Why is Ricardo so set on us? Your husband has never met either of us." It felt weird to use the term husband with his ex-partner, particularly because Blake had sworn when they were together that marriage was only for straight people.

"I know," Blake said. "I told him about you soon after I met you, and what you are doing now, and he has gotten it into his head that you are the only bodyguards he trusts, because of your past relationship with me."

Aidan caught a glimpse of his reflection in the window of the restaurant. He had aged since he'd left Blake; his brown hair had gray strands, and there were laugh lines around his mouth. He wasn't the cute young thing Blake had picked up at a gay bar in Philadelphia anymore. He'd left that man behind years before.

It was clear that Blake was still the take-charge guy he had been when he and Aidan broke up. It was going to take bluntness to get through to him.

"We aren't bodyguards anymore, Blake. We left the Agence de Sécurité a year ago and started a security advisory firm with two friends. We have clients and projects, and we can't drop them and head across the Atlantic because your husband is nuts."

"I will make it worth your while," Blake said. "Please, Aidan? For old times' sake?"

"Which old times are those? When you came home from work one day and said that things weren't working out between us and you told me to get out? Those times?"

"That was a mistake, and I've already apologized for it." Indeed, Blake had gone so far as to use a law school friend in the State Department to track Aidan to Liam's house in Tunis. Then he had shown up there to collect Aidan, as if he was a child who'd missed the school bus and needed to be picked up.

"We had good times," Blake continued. "Think of all the classes I paid for and the expensive gifts I bought you."

"You sent me to those classes so I could learn to cook for you and your guests. So I could arrange flowers to suit you, give you professional-quality massages. Does Ricardo do all of that?"

"Ricardo has his own career. He's a very important man."

"You mean he's as pompous as you are? I can't think of anything worse that spending a few days cooped up in a hotel room with you and a clone of you."

"Fine. I thought I could count on you, after all I did for you for eleven years. I guess I was wrong."

Blake ended the call abruptly. Aidan put the phone down and shook his head. Leopards never change their spots. As long as they both lived, Blake would think he could snap his fingers and Aidan would come running.

He couldn't help wondering, though, how Blake had aged. Even in his thirties, he'd used skin conditioners, gotten regular manicures and pedicures, and applied a variety of products to his thinning hair in the vain hope of preventing baldness. He had been addicted to his exercise bike, spending hours pedaling while reviewing law journals, and tracked his body mass index on a fancy scale.

Aidan had secretly smirked at his efforts. But maybe if Aidan had paid more attention to his own appearance back then, Blake would never have kicked him out.

That was a bad angle to think about. He loved his life, loved Liam with his whole heart, and could only appreciate the twists of fate that had brought them together.

He stared at the rippling Mediterranean in front of him, and let his mind go back to Blake. He did owe his ex a debt of gratitude, though in a different way than Blake thought. If Blake hadn't kicked him to the curb, Aidan would never have fled Philadelphia, landed in Tunis, and seen Liam showering naked behind the Bar Mamounia. Or accompanied Liam on a crazy adventure in the desert, fallen in love with him and then joined him in his bodyguard protection business.

But that was all in the past, he reminded himself. A year before, Liam had fallen from a ladder and broken his arm, and that had caused a crisis of confidence. They were both getting older, and close protection was a young man's game. They had taken advantage of an offer from their friends Louis and Hassam to start a business together.

Louis, a former CIA operative, advised companies on global threats, while Hassam, an architect, designed facilities that protected and tracked the movement of employees and data. Liam trained senior staff to avoid personal risk, and Aidan developed and taught courses that put all that information together.

He liked his work; he had a graduate degree in Teaching English as a Second Language, and he had been an instructor back in Philadelphia. The courses he designed and taught kept him in touch with students and the joy he found in communicating new concepts to them. He missed the drama of close protection work, but he had followed Liam's lead in putting that career behind him.

Was he repeating the same pattern with Liam that he'd established with Blake? He had agreed to become a bodyguard in the first place to spend more time with Liam. When Liam decided to leave Tunis for France, Aidan had followed. And Liam was the one who had proposed.

He frowned. He was being stupid. He was the one who had pressed to join Liam in close protection, though Liam had protested. He had been unhappy and worried in Tunisia, fearing the Arab country might turn against him as an American, a Jew, and a gay man, and Liam was the one who had volunteered to give up his home, his life and his contacts to move somewhere Aidan might feel safer.

The proposal had surprised him, though. He loved Liam with all his heart, and was envious of Louis and Hassam when they married, but Liam's parents' marriage had been a disaster, and Liam had always said he thought of marriage as an institution – and who wanted to be institutionalized?

That reminded him of Blake and Ricardo. How did Blake feel when Ricardo had to be hospitalized? Was it an annoyance, or had he finally learned to put someone else first? It was a tantalizing question, but not worth flying across the world to answer.

When Liam returned from his run, he was drenched in sweat, and though Aidan wanted to tell him about Blake's call, Liam immediately stripped off his shoes and socks and walked over to the outdoor shower.

Though Liam kept his shorts on, Aidan couldn't help remembering the first glimpse he'd had of Liam, nearly nine years before. Aidan had fled from Blake's rejection and accepted the first job he was offered, a teaching appointment in Tunis. While he waited to meet with his new boss, he had spent hours walking through the old city, then fleeing a couple of would-be robbers into a bar.

While he caught his breath, he'd looked out the rear window to the courtyard behind it—and seen Liam at an outdoor shower like this one. He had been mesmerized by Liam's body.

Now, though, he couldn't concentrate on Liam, and it wasn't just that he had seen that body naked nearly every day for the past nine years. He kept thinking about Blake. Blake said that Aidan and Liam were the only bodyguards that Ricardo could trust—but could Aidan trust that Blake was telling the truth?

3 – Bossy Husbands

Liam returned from his shower with a fresh towel wrapped around his waist and reclined on the chaise-longue beside Aidan. "Think we could get another round of those drinks?"

Aidan waved to the server and twirled his finger. Then he turned back to Liam.

"What did Blake want?" Liam asked.

"He wants to hire us." He explained about Ricardo's paranoia and his need for bodyguards at the conference in Nassau. "Do you believe Blake's nerve? As if we'd drop everything to look after him and his husband."

"And you're not interested in a vacation in the Bahamas?" Liam asked. "That's not like you."

Aidan stared at him. "You think a couple of days cooped up in a hotel with my ex and his paranoid husband would be a vacation? Are you on drugs?"

The server arrived with their drinks, and Liam raised his to Aidan's. As the glasses clinked, Liam asked, "Do you ever miss it? The adrenaline rush of protecting a client?"

Aidan's first reaction was to say not in the least. But he held his tongue and thought about it. "I like helping people," he said. "And we've been able to do some good in the world."

Most of their assignments had been routine – waiting outside hotel rooms for clients to finish meetings, shepherding them around and keeping an eye open for threats which never materialized. But some of their jobs had resulted in real change – bringing together couples, rescuing clients from danger, even shutting down a prison for gay men in Chechnya.

"But you said yourself we're getting too old for this," Aidan continued. "And I worry about you, even though I know you can handle any situation." He looked at his husband. "How about you? Do you miss it?"

Liam nodded. "I do. I love our life, working with you every day, advising clients. But I spent a long time as a bodyguard, and I miss being able to use my skills in a more tactile, hands-on way."

A gust of wind swept through the pool area, and a broken palm front slapped noisily against the tree's trunk. Aidan stared at Liam. "You'd take on this job, even knowing the history between me and Blake?"

Liam cocked his head slightly. "Are you suggesting I should be worried about putting the two of you together again?"

"Only that I might murder him," Aidan said. "You're not even a little jealous?"

Liam laughed as a couple of small children raced past on their way to the water. "In all the time we've been together, I think you've maybe said one or two nice things about Blake. Am I jealous that you might decide to go back to him? Not a chance. But you have to admit, you still have some issues with Blake. This might be a chance to put those to rest."

The cloud that had been blocking the sun moved away, and the rays blasted Aidan's skin, a contrast to the chilled glass he held in his hand.

"If we decide to take on this assignment, I'm only doing it under the auspices of the Agence," he said. "I don't want to get stuck chasing after Blake for payment if Ricardo suddenly changes his mind."

"That's a good idea. When does he need us?"

"The conference starts Monday and runs until Thursday."

Liam whistled. "Not much advance notice, is there? I don't have anything going on at work. Do you?"

The company they had founded with Louis and Hassam went through ups and downs. Things had been slow for the last month as Hassam finished construction drawings for a client. He hadn't had the time to scout for a new project, and though there would be more work for Louis, Liam and Aidan once the facility was under construction, they had little on their plates.

"I can get away," Aidan said. "I'm almost finished with a training course and I have nothing beyond that besides some emails to handle."

"Why don't we head home, and you can call Blake and figure out the details," Liam said. "You said Ricardo will only trust us. Let's see if we can trust him."

They returned to the Jeep, but Aidan was too filled with thoughts of Blake to pay attention to the scenery. Who was this Ricardo, who had managed to snare the commitment-phobic Blake into a marriage? Blake had only described him as an Argentine diplomat working in Philadelphia. How old was he? Was he handsome? Was he as disinterested in sex as Blake had been?

He stopped himself there, as Liam turned off the A8 highway and onto the local road that would lead them up into the hills toward Banneret. Blake's sex life with Ricardo was none of his business, and so was how the Argentine had convinced Blake to marry him.

But then, Liam had been as vocal against marriage until he broke his arm and came to see how much he and Aidan loved and depended on each other. Perhaps Blake had experienced the same thing with Ricardo.

They pulled up in front of their renovated stone farmhouse, and Aidan opened the front door, immediately assailed by the small, lion-faced Hayam, eager to see her daddies but at the same time angry she'd been left behind. Liam ferried the two boxes of wine inside as Aidan gave the dog a treat. Then Aidan settled at the dining room table with his laptop open and called Blake.

His ex was as bossy as ever. "You'll meet us the condo," Blake said, as soon as Aidan told him that he and Liam had accepted the job. "Ricardo will be much more comfortable traveling with you."

Aidan agreed because Blake was paying the bills. The conference was to begin on Monday morning at nine AM, so that meant an early afternoon flight from Nice to London and then a transfer, arriving in Philadelphia on Saturday evening. They'd stay at a hotel, then travel to the airport together Sunday morning.

Blake was as detail-oriented as Aidan remembered. He knew what was scheduled every moment of the conference, where they would eat and when they would sneak away to shop in Nassau. Liam was as careful, particularly when it came to protecting a client, but somehow he wasn't as irritating about it as Blake.

It would still be a tight schedule, and after Aidan hung up, he considered how he and Liam would feel after a fourteen-hour flight, jet lag and a six-hour time difference. He made an executive decision on his own, to fly in on Friday instead of Saturday. That would give him and Liam a chance to rest and get acclimated. And maybe he could take a short trip down memory lane, checking out places he had lived and worked. He hadn't been back to Philadelphia since his quick exit from Blake's apartment, and he was eager to see how things had changed.

He got up and walked into the bedroom, unsure of what to do next. His mind was filled with so many memories, he almost felt dizzy. He sat on the bed as Liam walked in. "I put all the bottles into the wine storage unit," he said.

He looked at Aidan. "What's the matter?"

Aidan shrugged. "I don't know if this is a good idea. Going back to Philadelphia, seeing Blake, stirring up so many ghosts."

"I know how to take your mind off your troubles."

In one smooth motion Liam pulled off his polo shirt, and his nipple rings glinted in a slice of sunshine. Then he kicked off his deck shoes and dropped his shorts, leaving him in a jockstrap so white it glowed. His ample dick pressed against the fabric, hardening as Aidan watched, like a snake preparing to strike.

Once again, Aidan's marveled at how handsome his husband was. Even after years out of the Navy, he had maintained his military-grade figure. His waist was still trim though there was perhaps an ounce or two of fat above the hips—his fault, he knew, because he was always tempting Liam with rich foods and desserts.

"Why are you still dressed?" Liam demanded, his hands on his hips.

Aidan sprawled back against the covers. "Because I want you to undress me."

"The things I do for love," Liam grumbled. But he did lean down and pull off Aidan's deck shoes.

"The actual quote is the things *WE* do for love," Aidan said. "10CC. Released the year I was born."

Liam sat on the bed with Aidan's bare feet in his lap. "How in the world do you know things like that?"

"It used to be a thing: people would give you these birthday cards with who else was born in that year, what the popular books and movies were."

Liam massaged Aidan's left foot, pulling apart the toes and pressing his knuckles into the sole. "And what movie was popular then?"

"*Rocky* was number one," Aidan said, his breath catching as Liam rubbed his big strong hand over his metatarsals. "I didn't see it until I was a teenager, but man, Stallone rocked that body."

"Hmm. You like big, muscular guys?" Liam pulled Aidan forward and snaked his hand beneath Aidan's shorts and boxers.

"I used to jerk off to a photo of David Hasselhoff from *Baywatch*," Aidan said. "He was wearing a black jockstrap and looking right into the camera like he wanted me."

Liam snickered. "And your parents didn't know you were gay

then?" He squeezed Aidan's dick in his meaty hand.

"It wasn't a poster on the wall. A picture I ripped out of a magazine."

Liam thumbed the top of Aidan's dick and Aidan asked, "Who did you jerk off to?"

"I admit I had a thing for Marky Mark and his funky bunch," Liam admitted. He let go of Aidan's dick and used both hands to tug down the shorts and boxers. "I wouldn't have minded getting between him and his Calvins."

Once Aidan's dick was free, Liam leaned down and took it in his mouth.

"Oh, yeah," Aidan said. "I'm seeing teenaged Liam, lying on that single bed of yours, your hand wrapped around your dick, staring goggle-eyed at Marky Mark."

Liam didn't respond, just continued sucking Aidan's dick. Aidan pulled up his shirt, exposing his abs, and then caressed Liam's dirty blond locks. He no longer wore the high-and-tight of the military, so it was long enough for Aidan to wrap his fingers around a few strands.

Liam backed off and stood. "Hold that pose."

Aidan watched while Liam shucked his jockstrap and his big dick bounced. Liam grabbed a bottle of lube from the bedside table and returned to the bed. He climbed up on his knees as Aidan pulled off his shirt and then scooted forward.

"That's it, come to Papa," Liam said.

Liam lubed up his index finger and stuck it into Aidan's ass, and Aidan drew in a quick breath. "Oh yeah," he said.

Liam poked and twisted his finger until it reached Aidan's prostate. Aidan felt boneless already, his whole body a single guitar string ready to be twanged. "It's about time I funk you, baby," Liam said, making no attempt to sing the lyrics that Mark Wahlberg made famous.

"Then do it," Aidan said.

"Pushy bottom," Liam grumbled. "It's all about you, isn't it?"

"If will be if you get your dick in me."

Liam grabbed the bottle again and lubed up his dick. They had long since stopped using condoms, having made a commitment to fidelity within weeks of meeting. He grabbed Aidan's legs with his oily hands and positioned himself at Aidan's hole. And then, in one quick and blessed movement, he was inside.

This was love, and marriage, and everything that came with it, Aidan thought. This connection with his partner, his love, his husband. Feeling Liam like a part of him.

Then Liam began his in and out movement, and Aidan lost the ability to think, only to feel Liam's dick inside him, his hands on Aidan's thighs, to smell Liam's breath, still grapefruit-scented.

He banged his head back against the pillow as Liam slammed into him. "I'm getting close, baby," Liam said. "You want to join me?"

"Oh, yeah."

Liam released his grasp on one of Aidan's thighs and wrapped his right fist around Aidan's dick. He began jerking it in the same rhythm he used to plunder Aidan's ass, and the endorphins kept rising in Aidan's blood, wiping out anything except this connection, this man, this dick inside him ready to blow.

Liam shot off in Aidan's ass in a hot, solid spurt. Aidan yipped and mumbled some incoherent syllables, and then he fell over the edge, too, shooting his come so hard it nearly reached his pecs, then began dribbling down his stomach.

Liam held his pose for an extra minute, Aidan savoring the connection between them, before pulling out and sprawling beside Aidan. He kissed Aidan's cheek, and then he was out cold.

Aidan fell asleep a few minutes later and napped for nearly two hours. By the time he woke darkness had fallen, and Hayam was eager for her dinner. He left Liam asleep in bed, cleaned his belly and groin, put on his boxers, and walked to the kitchen with the small dog.

He poured kibble in her bowl, and after she scarfed it down he opened the back door to let her run out into the garden there.

There were definite benefits to having a bossy husband, he thought. He was grateful that the man who was bossing him around was no longer Blake. Ricardo could have him, and Aidan hoped, in a way that surprised him, that they were as happy as he and Liam were.

4 – True Confessions

The following week moved quickly. Aidan finished the training course he was working on and submitted it to the client. Then he and Liam both wrapped up small details, preparing for ten days away from the business. They arranged for Hayam to stay next door with their friends Slava and Thierry, who they knew would spoil the little dog.

Thursday evening, they packed. When he decided to join Liam in his personal protection business, Aidan had taken a weeklong course in Georgia on the basics of the job. He'd come home with lists of items to have on hand for a wide range of assignments, including a long-handled inspection mirror used to look under vehicles for bombs, two-way radios and a charging station, folding knives, and an emergency medical kit.

He couldn't take everything with them, but there was still a wide range of gadgets to pack into the two big duffel bags and the matching backpacks they used for travel.

Aidan had spent years packing Blake's bag for travel, and he kept a regular stock of travel-sized deodorant, shampoo, and other grooming products on hand. He knew how to roll clothes to minimize wrinkles, what items could do double duty, and a dozen other arcane tips.

Liam had taught Aidan to pack so that the most necessary items were easily accessible. They carried a handheld GPS, useful in unfamiliar locales. Pocket knives, an emergency medical kit, a digital tape recorder and high-quality camera, their laptops, and other computer gear. Not to mention chargers for everything.

Liam had also taught Aidan to put things in the same place every time—even something as simple as a dopp kit always on the right side at the bottom. Aidan's bag was packed the same way so that in a crisis, either of them could find what they needed in either bag.

They would not be able to take their guns with them; they were not licensed law enforcement, and Liam believed that proper close protection procedures kept the client far enough from harm that weapons were not necessary.

Aidan began with their clothes, while Liam organized the equipment. Liam was much broader in the chest than Aidan, but he liked his shirts tight, and Aidan preferred his loose. That meant they could share those, as well as cargo shorts, with multiple pockets for phones, flashlights, and other tools of their trade. Since Liam was several inches taller, with bigger feet, the only clothes they couldn't switch off were slacks and shoes.

Friday morning. Louis arrived to take them to the airport in Nice. He pulled a sheaf of papers from the front seat, and as Liam slid in beside him, Louis handed the papers to him. "Bahamas Travel Advisory," he said. "Including some information the State Department doesn't release to ordinary citizens."

"Thanks, Louis. That's great."

From the back seat, Aidan tried to look over Liam's shoulder, but his partner flipped through the pages too quickly. "Level two alert," Liam read from the page. "The U.S. Department of State has assessed Nassau as being a critical-threat location for crime directed at or affecting official U.S. government interests."

"Your client isn't a U.S. official, is he?" Louis asked.

Liam shook his head. "But there will be a lot of government officials from various countries at this event. Hopefully there will be professional-level security."

He continued to read as Louis drove. "Lots of skimmer use in Nassau," he said. "We'll have to make sure to tell Blake and Ricardo it's not safe to use ATMs because of that, and to take whatever cash they need with them, preferably in a traveler's vest."

He flipped through the rest of the pages. "The good news is that most crime takes place against Bahamians in areas outside of tourist activity, and that areas with a lot of tourists have a high police presence. That will make it tougher for anyone to get at Ricardo if we leave the hotel."

"You believe your client is in danger?" Louis asked. "I thought you said he was nuts."

"He had a psychotic break a few months ago, and he's heavily medicated, according to Aidan's ex," Liam said. "But we have to treat every client as if the threat is real."

While they waited at a light, Louis twisted around to look at Aidan. "How do you feel about seeing the ex? Little nostalgia for what's lost?"

"Not at all," Aidan said. "If anything, talking to Blake during this past week has reminded me of everything that irritated me about him. And of how lucky I am that he kicked me out and I found Liam."

Louis stuck his finger in his mouth and mimed throwing up.

"Oh, come on, you're as much a romantic as any of us," Aidan said, knocking Louis in the shoulder. "I saw what you gave Hassam for your anniversary."

"What was that?" Liam asked. "Tell me it wasn't some kind of sex toy."

Now it was Liam's turn to get a knock on the shoulder. "It's a picture of the constellations in the sky the night they met," Aidan said. "Totally romantic."

Aidan sat back against the seat. "How did you guys meet? By the time big, cute and clueless in the front seat figured out you were gay, you and Hassam were already a long-term item."

"We met, that's all."

Aidan knew there was more to that.

"He's blushing, Aidan." Liam elbowed Louis. "Come on, fess up."

"I wasn't exactly closeted at work, but I wasn't completely out, either," Louis said, as the A8 turned south, along the River Var. They were in an industrial area, with the Allianz stadium and a *hypermarché* on the east side of the river, and fields on the other side tamped down for winter. "I had to be very discreet about dating—usually quick encounters where no names were exchanged."

"But there was something different about Hassam," Aidan said.

"You are such a romantic sap," Liam said. "Let the man tell his story."

"I went to a sleazy club late one night. Hassam was there in a tank top and skin-tight shorts." He was quiet. "We were both a lot younger then, and he was like sex on steroids. I couldn't wait to get my hands on him. I didn't even have to buy him a drink—I walked up to him, and a minute later I was groping him through those shorts."

"Wow." Aidan was getting hard imagining the scene.

"It was a pretty sleazy bar, and within a couple of minutes I had Hassam turned around up against the wall, his shorts down, a condom out and my dick inside him."

"And then?" Aidan asked.

"What do you think?" Liam said. "My guess is that Louis shot a load of come up Hassam's ass."

"Inside the reservoir of the condom, if you please," Louis said.

"You know that wasn't what I meant," Aidan said. "How did you get from a quick fuck in a bar to a lifetime together?"

"My usual pattern was to shoot off and then run out," Louis said. "But there was something different about Hassam. I turned him around, got down on my knees on that scummy bar floor and blew him, and then I was hooked."

He turned into the departure lane of the airport. "And thus ends our True Confessions for today. There's the entrance for your airline."

Aidan had to adjust himself in his pants before he got out. Then he slung his backpack on, hoisted his duffel over his shoulder, and led the way to the check-in counter.

They checked the pair of duffels and passed through the security checkpoint. As they walked to the gate, Liam said, "You love all that romantic stuff, don't you?"

"You know that I do. The vision of you showering naked behind the Bar Mamounia is imprinted on my brain, and not just because you were hella sexy back then."

"Back then!" Liam said with outrage. "I'm still hella sexy."

"You are, sweetheart," Aidan said, with enough of an edge of sarcasm to keep Liam on his toes.

"How did you and Mr. Attorney-with-a-stick-up-his-butt meet?"

"He didn't have a stick up his butt," Aidan said. "Nothing up his butt, if you know what I mean. Blake didn't swing that way."

"Only a top?"

"Strictly oral and hand jobs," Aidan said. "Even with a shower and a douche, an ass was too dirty for him."

"What a loser," Liam said. "Missing out on half the fun." They came to their gate and slung their packs on a seat. "But you're avoiding the question. How did you meet?"

"The usual way. At a bar. But a much nicer bar than the one where Louis met Hassam. No furtive sex in back rooms."

"Sounds boring."

"It was a piano bar," Aidan admitted.

"Really? A piano bar? And you were how old?"

"Twenty-three. A friend and I went there looking for sugar daddies."

"And you found Blake."

"Who was much more of a sweet and low daddy in the end. He was almost thirty, starting to lose his hair, but he wore this suit that had been tailored to fit him perfectly, and a handmade shirt in a light blue and white pinstripe, with a gold collar pin and a navy tie."

"And?" Liam sat on the hard plastic seat and spread his legs.

"He caught my eye right away. I was back in Philly after a year teaching English in Thailand, and I was broke and looking for someone to buy me a drink. I meandered over in his direction, and he reached out to shake my hand. He introduced himself and gave me his business card, in between 'I heard it through the grapevine' and 'Please, Mr. Postman.'"

Liam snorted with laughter. "He gave you his business card at a gay bar."

"Well, at least it meant he wasn't in the closet at work," Aidan said. "Or that's what I thought it meant. Turns out he was a lot like Louis back then. It was okay for people to know he was gay, but not to see anyone he was actually having sex with."

"He kept you in the closet?"

"For the first year. Then I was living with him, and he wanted to entertain clients, so he sent me to cooking school. The first few dinners he introduced me as his personal chef, but that didn't fool anybody, so the ruse didn't last long."

Aidan sat beside Liam, their legs touching. That first year had been a tough one. He had been falling in love with Blake but wasn't sure if Blake felt the same way. Every time Blake went to a business dinner on his own, or prevaricated about Aidan's position in his life, Aidan felt a knife stab into him. It wasn't until shortly after their first anniversary, when Blake invited him to a client dinner, that he finally felt things were settled between them.

That is, until that night that Blake came home and told him to move out.

5 – Fruitcake

The flight to Heathrow was quick and easy, and they were able to spend some time browsing the duty-free shops. Aidan was fascinated by the range of goods, everything from $5,000 watches to octagonal boxes of Caribbean rum cakes, and he browsed all kinds of things he couldn't carry with him like high-end scotch, sunglasses and beauty products.

Even with all that shopping, they made it to their flight to Philadelphia with plenty of time to spare. The flight was under-booked, and Liam got to stretch out in the aisle seat as he liked, while Aidan had the window. The long flight gave him lots of time to think about Blake Chennault.

He was more curious than he was willing to admit to Liam about Ricardo Levy. Was he better-looking than Aidan? Was he a better companion at dinner parties? Wealthy in his own right?

He had done his due diligence on Ricardo—as much as he'd do for any client, he convinced himself. Ricardo David Levy Fainshtain had been born in Buenos Aires in 1964. He had graduated from the University of Buenos Aires and then the London School of Economics, where he received his Masters of Science in Global Politics.

He returned to Buenos Aires then, and worked in various government departments for three years, until he was appointed an economic officer for the Argentine embassy in Tel Aviv. He worked there for ten years until Nestor Kirchner took over as president of Argentina and reorganized the embassy staff.

In 2003, Ricardo returned to Buenos Aires and joined the staff of *Capital Empresarial*, an NGO aimed at increasing entrepreneurship in South America. He stayed there for two years, and then there was a year-long gap in his resume. In 2006 he joined the Foreign Policy Research Institute in Philadelphia, and had remained there ever since.

There were still so many questions to be asked. How had he and Blake met? When had they married? What had Ricardo been doing during that year-long gap on his resume?

And was he crazy, or was there a justification for his fear?

As they landed in Philadelphia, he pulled on a sweater and took his leather jacket out of his pack. Liam did the same. The terminal was cold, and Aidan shrugged on the jacket, though he noticed Liam carried his. They collected their bags and went through Customs, then called for an Uber.

When they stepped out of the terminal, the bitter cold was a reminder to Aidan of how temperate the climate was back in Banneret-les-Vaux. A layer of snow remained on the center island and he was careful to stick to the cleared sidewalk as they walked to the Uber.

The driver dropped them at the hotel Blake had reserved for them in center city, a few blocks from his apartment. Aidan had extended the reservation without notifying Blake. If he knew, Aidan was sure he'd come up with additional demands, and Aidan wanted time to show Liam the city.

It was early afternoon, but felt much later in the day to them. Aidan took Liam on a walking tour of Rittenhouse Square, where he'd often met with students on warm days, pointing out the English words for everything from squirrel to bench to mini-skirt.

Many of the old buildings in the neighborhood were the same, though the piano bar where he had met Blake had been razed and replaced by a glassy condo tower. Despite the cold, the streets were busy with commuters hurrying home, buses traveling in packs on Walnut and Chestnut Streets, young singles buying dinner from gourmet delis.

They took another Uber later to South Philadelphia, so Aidan could introduce Liam to real Philly cheese steaks. The rich spray cheese oozed out of the just-baked bun, past the tender meat and sautéed mushrooms. "This is heaven." Aidan sighed. "I didn't realize how much I had missed these."

"So *soupe a l'oignon*, *boeuf bourgignon*, and *mousse au chocolat* don't do it for you anymore?"

Aidan was impressed at the way his partner's accent had improved over the years. When they first moved to Nice, Aidan had been the fluent one, while Liam spoke excellent Arabic and basic French. "*Mais oui, monsieur*," Aidan said. "But a good cheese steak…" He shook his head. "There's no comparison."

They returned to the hotel in another Uber and went to sleep soon after. Liam was up at sunrise, in sweatpants and an old Penn sweatshirt Aidan had held onto since college. "I'm going for a run," Liam said.

Aidan looked up the weather on his phone as Liam pulled on wool socks and sneakers. "It's thirty-two degrees out."

"Yes, the temperature at which water turns to ice," Liam said.

"Also known as zero degrees Centigrade. I'm getting soft, Aidan. I need to toughen up."

"Be my guest. Just don't catch a cold."

Aidan turned over and went back to sleep. Liam returned nearly an hour later, shivering with the cold yet exuberant. "Get up, sleepyhead. There must be more of this city we can see before we have to meet Blake and Ricardo."

They called another Uber to take them up to West Philadelphia, where they had breakfast at a café with a faux-European ambiance, even though cafés in Europe were nothing like the ones in the U.S. The sun was out and it had warmed up a few degrees, so Aidan led Liam on a quick tour of the Penn campus, pointing out the dorms where he had lived, the theater where he had worked as an usher. They stopped at the university bookstore and Aidan treated himself to a polo shirt and a pair of gym shorts, both with the university crest, a dolphin between a pair of books over a triangle featuring three balls. He couldn't remember what it all meant, but it was a comforting reminder of the happy years he had spent on the campus.

They had to scramble to get back to the hotel, pack up and check out. Blake had sent a limo to pick them up, because Ricardo was only willing to travel with a company he trusted and a driver he knew. Aidan called Blake as they pulled up in front of the high-rise building he had called home for nearly eleven years.

The trees out front were taller, and the lobby had been renovated, with new floor-to-ceiling windows. "Bad layout for a guy in danger," Liam said. "You could stake out an area right across the street, track his progress from the elevator through the lobby, then shoot right as he walked outside."

"Try not to mention that to Ricardo," Aidan said.

He watched as the elevator doors opened and Blake stepped out. The years had not been kind to him—his hair was sparser, more gray than brown, and despite all those fancy face creams he had lines across his forehead and around his mouth. Aidan was surprised Blake hadn't sprung for Botox.

He had put on some weight, too. He'd been almost painfully thin when Aidan lived with him, a picky eater who never finished what was on his plate, despite how delicious it was, and eschewed desserts. His camel hair trench coat, which Aidan remembered clearly, was tight around the stomach.

Ricardo looked older than Aidan expected, too, and taller as well. Blake was five-ten, and Ricardo looked at least three or four inches taller, though he walked with a slight hunch, as if embarrassed by his height. His curly black hair was immaculately cut, something he had in common with Blake, and he had heavy dark eyebrows.

His mouth was set in a grim line as he and Blake dragged their rollaboard cases out of the elevator. Blake carried a suit bag—not surprising to Aidan, who had packed that same bag many times. Even on vacation Blake wore dress pants and starched shirts. Ricardo had a messenger bag slung over his shoulder.

Aidan jumped out to help them, with Liam behind him. They made quick introductions in the marble-floored lobby. Blake reached out a hand to shake Aidan's, and Aidan was tempted to pull him into a hug—just because. But he shook Blake's hand, and then Ricardo's, and Liam did the same. Then Liam took both cases out to the limo, with Ricardo by his side.

"He's huge," Blake said, nodding toward Liam. "I can see why he works as a bodyguard."

"It takes more than size and strength to work in close protection," Aidan said, holding back his annoyance at Blake's rudeness. Clients needed education, and Blake was a client. "You need to plan strategies to reduce the opportunity for anyone to get to your client, be aware of a dozen details and keep an eye out for all kinds of dangers."

Blake ignored the information, as he always had done with material he thought was useless. "You look good, Aidan," he said, as they walked outside, where the cold air slammed into them once again like a closing door. Because they were busy getting into the limo, Aidan avoided having to lie by repeating the compliment.

Liam tried to engage Ricardo in conversation about the conference, but Ricardo nodded toward the driver and pursed his lips closed. They sat in an uncomfortable silence, Blake and Ricardo on the back seat and Liam and Aidan facing them, as the driver drove out of center city and onto the Schuylkill Expressway.

The skyline had changed but the Schuylkill River beside them was the same, flat and still. Only a single barge disturbed the placid surface. *A good metaphor for life,* Aidan thought, *and this trip in particular.* On the surface things were safe and simple, but who knew what currents lay beneath?

"Ricardo and I will go through the security checkpoint when we arrive," Liam said. "Aidan, you and Blake can handle the luggage."

Aidan expected Blake to blow up at that, but instead Blake said, "Good idea. Get Ricardo through the crowd as quickly as possible."

Liam slipped on his backpack and took his duffel and Blake's suit bag and still managed to have a hand free to gently guide Ricardo toward the TSA line. Ricardo kept his messenger bag over his arm.

Aidan pulled on his backpack and took his duffel in one hand, and Ricardo's hard-sided suitcase in the other, leaving Blake only his own rolling case. Aidan pushed forward to the bag check kiosk, awkwardly juggling the bags. He reminded himself that he was the hired help, and even when he and Blake had traveled together, he'd handled all the luggage. Things didn't change, and neither did people.

After Liam and Ricardo were gone, Aidan and Blake waited in line, Aidan asked, "Do you think there's a real threat against Ricardo at this conference? Or are you humoring him because of his mental state?"

Blake shrugged, but his body didn't relax; he was as tight as a guitar string. "It's hard to say. He has always been cagey about his past, but the break and the meds he's taking have accelerated that evasiveness into paranoia." He frowned. "He has hinted about some dark secrets in his past, but he's never been open with me. For example, I know when he left Argentina, but I don't know why."

"It wasn't to take the job in Philadelphia," Aidan said. "Because there was nearly a year's gap in his resume before he started there."

Blake looked surprised, as the line shuffled forward. "You know that?"

"Of course. Liam and I would never begin a case without knowing as much as possible about the client. Do you know what he did during that year?"

"He spent some time in Los Angeles and New York looking for work until he got the job with the Institute." Another clerk opened a podium, and the serpentine line moved forward quickly. Aidan had to push and pull the three suitcases without banging into the sari-clad woman in front of him.

"How did this illness begin to manifest itself?" Aidan asked.

"Ricardo started to get very stressed back in September, and I could tell something was wrong, but he insisted it was pressure at work. He was finishing a big research project and had to triple check all his sources."

"And then?"

"It kept getting worse. He began to be paranoid—we couldn't go out to dinner because he didn't want to be out after dark. He suspected people, even our oldest friends, of having ulterior motives."

"That must have been very hard for you, to see him get sicker and sicker." Aidan could only imagine. When Liam had fallen from the roof a year before, Aidan had freaked out at seeing him unconscious on the ground. Fortunately the result had only been a broken arm, and Liam had recovered quickly, without side effects.

"I've never experienced anything so terrible," Blake said. "I thought I was losing him, minute by minute. It's like the man I fell in love with and married was falling underwater, and I couldn't do anything to pull him out."

They reached the clerk and got claim checks for all the bags, then had to drag them to the scanning station. The lobby was crowded with vacationers heading to warm climates, businessmen and women traveling in logo-shirted packs, and families with young children in strollers and hanging in front of them in reverse backpacks. Every time people came in through the sliding doors a blast of cold air rolled through, and the loudspeaker kept repeating weather alerts and gate changes.

It wasn't until he and Aidan were in line for the TSA check that Blake spoke again. "I thought I was coping as things got worse and worse. Then Ricardo had this psychotic break, and I was completely lost." He started to shake, and Aidan put his arm around him.

It was a surprise that Blake let him do that. Blake had always been opposed to public displays of affection, but maybe since they were no longer lovers this kind of casual contact was more acceptable. "What happened?"

Blake straightened up, and Aidan pulled his arm back. "Ricardo was sure that the police were coming to arrest him, though he wouldn't tell me why. He insisted they were out in the hallway, and when I took him out there and showed him there was no one there, he said he would sit out there and wait for them."

Blake's words came out in a rush, as if this story was one he had kept bottled up until he had someone he could trust to tell it to. "I finally convinced him that he needed to go to the hospital so I called the limo company. And Brian, the same driver we had this morning, took us to HUP."

Aidan was quite familiar with the Hospital of the University of

Pennsylvania; he had gone to the student health office there when he was an undergraduate to get allergy shots, accompanied a friend with alcohol poisoning to the ER, and been at his mother's bedside when the cancer invading her body finally overcame her.

"The attending at the ER checked him out and admitted him to the psych ward," Blake said. "It was horrible, Aidan. It's a locked down unit and they only have limited visiting hours. I'd go to see Ricardo and he was like a stranger, nearly catatonic from the medication they gave him. He cried all the time."

"I feel terrible for both of you," Aidan said, as they moved forward in the long, curving line. "Eventually, they let him out?"

"His insurance only covered two weeks of psychiatric hospitalization. I brought him home, and he was in terrible shape, but at least the medication controlled his behavior. Still a lot of paranoia, and he didn't want to be left alone, so I took a family medical leave of absence from the law firm to look after him."

That was a huge surprise to Aidan. Blake had been completely dedicated to his career, at first striving to make partner, then when he had, focused on accumulating billable hours. He worked most Saturdays, answered emails on Sundays, traveled to conferences and client meetings. The idea that he'd walked away from that to play caregiver changed everything Aidan thought he knew about his former partner.

"I thought he was getting better when he insisted on going to this conference," Blake said. "But then he began micro-managing every detail."

Aidan couldn't help himself from laughing.

"I know, you think I do that," Blake said, with a grim smile. "But I've been different with Ricardo. He cares so much about those details that I let him have his head."

He shrugged. "Maybe a change of scene will make him feel better. And seeing a lot of people he's worked with in the past should be good, too."

"Whatever happens, Liam and I will look out for him," Aidan said. They moved through the TSA check and met Liam and Ricardo at the gate. They were sitting in a corner, their backs to the wall, Liam's backpack and suitcase and Blake's suit bag stacked in front of them like a protective wall. It was hard to say who was more vigilant of the two.

Blake had paid for priority boarding, but Ricardo insisted he didn't want to get on until everyone else was in place. Liam waited with him while Aidan and Blake took the backpacks and bags on and stowed them. Just before the pilot was ready to close the door, Ricardo and Liam got on.

It was a smaller jet, lines of two seats on either side of the aisle, and Aidan sat at the window with Liam on the aisle. Across from him was Ricardo, with Blake at the window. Ricardo didn't want to put his messenger bag under the seat in front of him, and Blake had to murmur quietly to him until he complied.

"This guy is nuttier than a fruitcake," Liam muttered to Aidan. "But like the saying goes, just because you're paranoid doesn't mean someone isn't out to get you."

6 – Amulets & Crystals

Liam did not like the airport in Nassau. It was too congested, filled with families with crying children, limo drivers waving signs and Bahamian dancers in feathered headdresses and brightly colored bikinis, shilling for change. An elderly Rastafarian man in a red, green and yellow knit cap held a hand-written sign that read, "Welcome to the Bahamas. Now go home." He wore a half-dozen rope chains around his neck bearing what looked like religious symbols, a cross and an ankh among them, though Liam thought he spotted Tweety Bird lurking behind a cluster of saints' medals.

Aidan was escorting Ricardo, and the client's visible agitation seemed to be making Aidan nervous, too. Liam needed his partner's full attention on the client and the surroundings, so he moved up to walk beside Ricardo, using his body language to shift Aidan to Blake.

"Calm down, Ricardo," Liam said as he joined him. "You aren't in the United States anymore. There's bound to be a bit more chaos than you're accustomed to."

"I come from a country which had six *coups d'etat* in the twentieth century," Ricardo said. "I know about instability and chaos. That does not mean I like it."

The pavement outside the airport was divided into three lanes—the closest for a taxi rank, the middle for through traffic, and the far lane for tour buses and SUVs. In practice, though, people simply stopped in each lane to load or unload passengers, so there was a lot of horn honking and very little movement.

They couldn't find the limo that Blake had reserved, and Ricardo didn't want to take a public bus. Poor Blake had to run up and down the congested driveway looking for a car to take them to the Atlantis Hotel, and he didn't have any luck. Liam walked up to the taxi dispatcher and palmed him an American twenty-dollar bill, and suddenly a cab was available for them.

They drove for quite a while on a highway. Liam reminded himself as they swerved through a roundabout that they were in a former British colony so they drove on the right, and the driver, a boy barely out of his teens, was not deliberately trying to kill them.

As they got into the urban part of Nassau, traffic was stop and go, and it looked like the driver wasn't sure where he was going. Every time he hesitated at a light or checked his GPS, Ricardo groaned. "Are we ever going to get there?" he asked.

"Soon come," the driver said. "Relax, mon. You on vacation now."

"No, I am not. And if you cannot get us to the hotel you had better call us someone who can."

Typical bossy client, Liam thought, and he was surprised at how upset the comment seemed to make Aidan. He remembered things Aidan had said over the years, about how difficult Blake had been, always needing everything to be exactly as he wanted. Had Ricardo learned that behavior from Blake? Or had they been attracted to each other in the way of the French proverb, *Qui se ressemble, s'assemble* – those who resemble each other assemble together?

Liam was surprised when he found their route took them right through downtown Nassau, onto Bay Street, five lanes of slow-moving cars, delivery trucks and tour buses. The streets were lined with linen shops, jewelry stores, and places selling T-shirts that changed color in the sun. It was easy to tell the locals from the tourists; the former were dark-skinned and dressed in business suits or hotel uniforms, while the latter were mostly white. The men wore garish T-shirts and cargo shorts and carried open bottles of beer or plastic cups, while the women wore too-small tops and flowing skirts over flip-flops.

It was a relief when they finally passed through the clogged downtown, though Liam wondered how much farther they had to go. He peered out the cab window and spotted the coral-pink towers of the hotel complex across a body of water, and kicked himself for not checking the map before leaving.

The vista from the outbound bridge was marvelous, an expanse of rippling green water dotted with sailboats. From the bridge they plunged into a tunnel, then drove slowly along streets lined with tall trees that cast dark shadows.

"You're sure this is the right place?" Blake demanded as they pulled up in an entrance plaza as wide as the lanes feeding into the Lincoln Tunnel. Bellhops in white uniforms laden with epaulets opened doors and took luggage.

"Yah, mon, Atlantis dis be," the driver said, and hopped out, eager to get rid of his passengers. He had their bags out on the pavement and was driving away before Blake could hail a bellman to help them.

It appeared that the taxi had dropped them off at the wrong tower for the huge hotel. The bellman was the same age as the driver, pimply and disinterested. He explained that he wasn't allowed to take bags to any of the other towers. "I can call you other cab, or you take bags yourself to Coral lobby to check in."

Liam got directions, and they began carrying and dragging their bags down the crowded hallways that linked the six different sections of the resort. *At least the hotel was lovely,* he thought, as they passed indoor waterfalls, displays of fresh flowers, and bronze statues of frolicking dolphins. Aidan would like that.

"I need to stop here," Ricardo said, as they passed a round pool with a mermaid statue in the center. He opened his shirt and pulled out a bunch of chains from which various rocks and emblems hung, like the Rastafarian man at the airport. He leaned down and dipped a clear crystal in the water and mumbled something.

Liam looked at Aidan but didn't say anything.

Then they continued to the next lobby, where they finally got a bell man to take their luggage up to the room. Ricardo insisted on carrying his messenger bag, refusing to let the young man put it on his cart.

The elevator lobby on the eighteenth floor featured a TV set and several couches, and a pair of kids were sitting there watching a cartoon. Three hallways led at angles from the lobby, and the bellman chose the one straight ahead of them.

He led them to the end of the hallway and opened the door into a small living room with a balcony overlooking the pool. One bedroom was to the left, the other to the right. No other tower faced them, so no one could get a shot into the room or at someone on the balcony. Good.

Blake tipped the bellman and he and Ricardo went into the bedroom to the right. Liam double-locked the front door and stood in the living room with Aidan.

"What do you think?" Aidan asked.

"Too many points of contact," Liam said. "Those long corridors between lobbies? Don't like them. There's no quick and easy way out of the hotel; you have to go through the registration lobby where there are dozens of people and too many places to hide."

"Well, we didn't pick this place, but we're stuck with it."

Aidan grabbed one duffel and Liam the other, and he followed Aidan into the second bedroom. There were two queen-sized beds in the room, which had another balcony that faced the ocean. He walked over to look outside.

The Atlantic was a brilliant blue-green, shading darker as it got deeper. A line of palm trees ran down the beach, where he saw kids and adults on the sand and in the water. A large, irregularly shaped pool was directly below them, with a shallow kiddie pool at one end and a spa pool at the other. Recliners lined the area, some of them occupied, others folded down on themselves. A beach hut at one end dispensed towels and sold beverages and snacks.

To one side, he saw the lazy river, where people got into big inner tubes and let the current float them along through a sort of jungle. Not a ride you'd put a client on, because they'd be too vulnerable to someone in the underbrush with a gun.

It was a shame to have to look at such a beautiful resort through the eyes of a bodyguard. It was so beautiful, organized for fun and relaxation, and it was spoiled by having to consider points of vulnerability, places where their client could be attacked or worse.

He turned to Aidan. "I saw an arrow toward the convention center when we walked in. At least it's in this tower. I want to go down and check it out. You'll be all right with the clients while I go?"

"Of course. I'll unpack and see what Blake has planned for the evening."

Liam had been in a lot of fancy hotels during his stint in close protection, and he could tell that this tower was older and in need of some renovation. The carpet was frayed in places, the paint chipped around the entrance to the maintenance room where the carts were stored.

There were only two elevators, which was a problem because of the wait involved and the chance that they'd be crowded into a cabin with strangers. The lobby area was well-maintained, though, and a careful sweep noted the presence of a security guard gossiping with a young woman at the excursions desk, and two more standing together in front of a gift shop specializing in native foods and crafts.

He walked up to the store window and pretended to be engrossed in the display of guava jelly and cans of a soda called Goombay Punch. "Big conference start tomorrow," the older guard said to the younger one. "Got to be on your game, my fellow."

"You think there be problems?" the younger man asked, in a thicker accent. Liam noticed that each of the staffers wore an oval tag with name and home island. Bertram, the older one, was from Turks & Caicos, while Promise, the younger, was from Eleuthera.

"A conference of Jews," Bertram said, his accent gentle and rolling. "Never know what kind of problem religious conferences bring, yah? Religion the cause of most of the problems in the world."

He nodded down the hall. "We have extra help from police from Nassau," he said, accenting the last syllable the way Liam had heard other natives do. "Keep everything calm."

They began walking down the hallway, and Liam couldn't follow them to continue to eavesdrop. But at least he felt comforted that the hotel security was preparing for the conference.

He followed signs down the hall to the convention center, but the door was locked. Another good idea, and he found himself approving of the way the hotel was handling things.

He walked around the entire lobby, checking nooks and crannies where bad guys could hang out. The line at customer service was long, where a young woman fielded complaints about hotel plumbing, rude lifeguards at the pool, and other sundry problems.

When he returned to the suite, Blake stood in front of a round table, laying out a dozen pills of varying shapes and sizes for Ricardo to take.

"I found a restaurant where we can have dinner," Liam announced. "No reservations required, but I can get us a table where we have a view of the only entrance, as well as the kitchen, with our backs to the wall."

"I don't want to go out," Ricardo said. "And I don't want to order room service."

He began to take the chains carrying the crystals from around his neck. There were at least six, some in silver, some in gold, some in rope. Several of them were tangled and he couldn't get them off.

"Let me help you." Blake began untying the chains and Liam was pleased to see a genuine kindness in Aidan's ex that he hadn't seen before.

"What do you want to eat?" Blake asked as unhooked the last chain and lifted the tangle over Ricardo's head.

"There are takeout restaurants in the market," Ricardo said. "Where they won't know who the food is for."

Liam shot Aidan a raised eyebrow, but his partner didn't respond. Or oops, his husband. He'd have to get used to that change of terminology, though perhaps it was best if he thought of Aidan as his partner when they were at work.

"There's a hotel magazine on the table," Aidan said, as Ricardo gobbled his pills with a tall glass of bottled water. He picked it up and flipped through it. "The take-out choices are a deli, a fifties-style diner and a pizzeria."

"This pizzeria, they have goat cheese and pesto?" Ricardo asked.

Aidan shook his head. "I think it's aimed at children who don't want to eat at the fancy restaurants. Cheese, mushroom, sausage or pepperoni."

"Cheese, then," Ricardo said.

"Sausage and mushroom for me." Blake finished untangling the chains and laid them out on the table separately. Liam was impressed at the variety of stones, the different colors, shapes and sizes. At the same time, he recognized that they weren't decoration; they were tied somehow into Ricardo's neurosis. How that played out remained to be seen.

7 – Handshake Your Fear

Aidan would have preferred something fancier than pizza, especially in a luxury hotel studded with star-chef restaurants serving seafood and local cuisine. At least one of the dining rooms was run by a chef Aidan had seen on the Food Network, though that didn't mean he was actually behind the stove.

The pizzeria didn't take online orders, so Aidan took the elevator down to the lobby, made a couple of wrong turns, and finally ended up outside. He had to turn again and walk down a broad set of stone steps to reach the marina, where the restaurants for those with simple palates were clustered.

Two teenaged boys rushed through the crowd and Aidan experienced a deep fear, struck by the way they resembled the thieves who had chased him through the streets of Tunis the day he met Liam. There was an almost palpable ripple of anxiety in the crowd as they passed, and Aidan half expected a security guard to appear in pursuit.

But the boys were only playing, and the crowd closed around them. Aidan took a couple of deep breaths and then walked into the pizzeria, where the familiar smells of dough, tomato sauce and cheese soothed him.

He waited in a long line for one pizza with sausage and mushrooms and one with cheese only, then carried them all the way back to the room, occasionally juggling them when his hands got too hot.

Blake ate one slice of pizza and then announced he was going into the bedroom to work. Ricardo ate most of the cheese pizza then followed him, and Aidan heard voices raised in there. He and Liam finished the rest of the two pizzas, while they tried not to intrude on their clients' privacy.

After they finished eating, Aidan left the pizza boxes outside in the hallway, and joined Liam in their bedroom. Liam went into the bathroom, and Aidan sat on the bed with the hotel magazine. He had only flipped through a couple of pages before he heard the door to the other bedroom slam.

He put down the magazine and walked out into the living room, to find Ricardo there. He was agitated, pacing around the room and stealing glances at his watch.

"What can I do to help you feel better?" Aidan asked.

Ricardo walked over to the sliding glass door, peered out, and then stepped back and turned to Aidan. "Did you love him?"

"You mean Blake?"

Ricardo nodded.

Aidan blew out a puff of air. "Yes, I did. At first it was infatuation. He was handsome and interested in me. So much more accomplished than I was at that time. And then, you know how it is. You spend enough time together and an affection develops. He broke my heart when he kicked me out."

"He says he was stupid to do that." Ricardo smiled. "But then, if he had not, I would not have met him."

"And I wouldn't have met Liam." Aidan directed the same question back to Ricardo. "Do you love Blake?"

"An affection has developed between us," Ricardo said. "In my country, you know, men do not love each other as they do with women."

"Of course they do," Aidan said. "Maybe they aren't open about it, but gay men are gay men, no matter what their culture. And you've lived outside Argentina for a long time."

"More than half my life," Ricardo admitted. "But what you learn as child, that forms your character."

Liam joined them in the living room, and Ricardo sat on the sofa. "I know I am having mental problems," he said. "But I have had real threats." He took a deep breath. "I did not want to tell Blake because I did not want to worry him."

Aidan thought that was laughable, because Blake was already as worried as he could possibly be about Ricardo's mental state. But in his experience, clients did not often behave rationally—especially if they were already upset.

"What kind of threats?" Liam asked. He and Aidan sat on the sofa across from Ricardo.

"The first ones came in the mail. Always a single sheet of paper, printed from a computer, with a message in large type."

"Did you save them?"

Ricardo shook his head. "I thought they were stupid, so I threw them away."

"Do you remember what the messages said?"

"Very vague things, like "forget what you know" or "you know nothing.""

"You have no idea what they were referring to?"

"At the time, I did not." He held his hands together, massaging them. "Then the phone calls began."

Aidan and Liam waited. Both of them knew the client would eventually tell them what he wanted, in his own time.

Finally, he looked up. "I was not a very religious child. My parents forced me to be a bar mitzvah, and that was that. I did not even enter a synagogue for more than a decade, until I was at school in London."

Aidan smiled and nodded, encouraging Ricardo to continue, even though they had probably strayed far from whatever was threatening him.

"I met a group of Orthodox Jews there and became more interested in religion. I studied Hebrew, and by the time I returned to Buenos Aires with my master's degree, I was fluent in the language."

Through the window Aidan saw the start of a fireworks display, bright flashes of red, green and blue against the dark sky behind Ricardo.

"I joined the diplomatic service and after a short time I was sent to the Argentine Embassy in Tel Aviv as an economic officer. Through my work, I met many people from companies and countries that wanted to do business with Argentina."

Aidan stole a glance at Liam. His posture was perfectly relaxed, as if Ricardo was simply telling them an interesting story.

"One of the men I worked with was a Persian Jew working in Tel

Aviv for a company headquartered in Tehran that exported nuts."

Aidan had to suppress a giggle. He finally was able to ask, "What kind of nuts?"

"Almonds, walnuts, macadamias, and cashews. As you probably know, the first two are particularly important in Israeli cuisine, in desserts and in rice dishes. So there could be a lucrative market, and he and I worked closely together."

The sound of small booms and cracks from the fireworks penetrated through the glass doors. Aidan felt the air in the room fizzle. There was a connection between Iran and Argentina that danced at the edge of his consciousness, but he waited for Ricardo to get there at his own pace.

Ricardo continued, "This man, he came to me one day, very upset. I had only been at my post for one year, maybe two. It was in 1995, I remember. On the anniversary of the AMIA bombing."

"The Jewish community center in Buenos Aires," Liam said. "I remember that. I was a Navy SEAL at the time, and one of my team members was Jewish. He was very upset about it."

Ricardo nodded sadly. "Yes, the bombing upset many people. Including my exporter friend. He came to me that day and said he had documentation that proved the Iranian government was behind the bombing, and he wanted to give it to me."

"What did you do?"

"Why, I accepted it, of course. And I passed it on to an intelligence agent. Then I waited to see the information become public."

"But it didn't," Aidan said. "The Iranian government was never formally charged, were they?"

"No, they were not. I waited patiently, nearly ten years. The government of my country changed, to President Kirchner, and I was called back to Buenos Aires and sidetracked in a minor ministry office. I kept trying to get my information heard, but the judge in the case was corrupt and refused to enter it into evidence. Then in 2004 all the suspects were found not guilty."

"That must have been very difficult for you," Aidan said.

It was. I became more and more vocal, and eventually I was fired and had to leave Argentina. I applied for asylum in the United States, and I moved around from place to place for the next year until it was granted. Then I was able to accept my current job in Philadelphia."

Aidan understood what it was like to lose everything you had. He had been lucky to find Liam so quickly, or he might have ended up like Ricardo, roaming the earth in search of a place to belong.

"Bring us up to the present," Liam said gently. "When did these threats begin?"

"In early September."

Aidan asked, "When did you accept this invitation to speak?"

"Almost a year ago."

That didn't jive with the onset of the threat. But Aidan knew that often the agenda for a conference wasn't revealed until much closer to the date. "When did the names of the speakers become public? Were you all listed in some brochure?"

"They did not release the agenda until September 1."

From the look on Ricardo's face, it appeared to Aidan that he made the connection at the same time that Aidan did. "The threats began once someone knew you were going to speak at this conference. Did the brochure list your interest in the AMIA bombing?"

"In a way. I published an article in a small journal a year ago, analyzing how the bombing had changed the attitudes of Jews in Argentina, and it was as a result of that article that I was invited to speak. My biography mentioned the article."

"Did you accuse the Iranians in this article?"

"Only in passing," Ricardo said. "Since the information I had was never made public, the peer reviewer insisted that I remove most of the references."

"Let's pull some of these threads together," Liam said. "Am I correct in stating that a year ago you published an article in which you mentioned that you had proof that the Iranian government was involved in this bombing?"

Ricardo nodded. The last of the fireworks splattered the sky behind him in a huge explosion of sparkles and showers of colored lights.

Liam seemed to be thinking out loud. "Then why didn't the threats begin then?"

"Publicity," Aidan said. "An article in an academic journal gets little notice. But a big conference like this one, dozens of speakers, gets much more attention."

Liam nodded. "That makes sense. The threats began after you were announced as a speaker, back in September. The threats continued throughout the fall?"

"Yes. By early November I had changed my phone number twice, but the calls kept coming through, warning me not to say anything, not to come to the Bahamas for this conference."

"And you didn't think of cancelling?" Aidan asked.

"I was not thinking clearly," Ricardo protested. "The stress was overwhelming, and when I went into the hospital on November fifteenth Blake took over managing my affairs."

Aidan leaned forward. "Did the phone calls continue?"

Ricardo shook his head. "Not that Blake ever told me."

"Perhaps whoever was behind them knew that you had been hospitalized. Did you tell your doctors about the threats you had been receiving?"

Ricardo shook his head.

"Why do the doctors think you had a breakdown?"

"They say it must have been stress."

"The stress from getting threatening messages and phone calls?" Aidan asked. "That sounds like something you should have told someone about."

Ricardo pulled his string of crystals from under his shirt and started fingering them. "Handshake your fear," he muttered. "This is only a distortion. With every breath, I feel myself relaxing."

He seemed to go into a trance. "Good job, Aidan," Liam muttered. "Push the client so far he goes nutty again."

"We have to know what he's up against," Aidan whispered. He turned to the client. "It's all right, Ricardo. Liam and I are here, and we're not going to let anything happen to you."

"With every breath I feel myself…" Ricardo got up and began pacing around the room. "These drugs," he said. "They make everything worse. I don't know how to stop the voices in my head."

Aidan stood and grabbed Ricardo's hand, stopping him from pacing. "Focus on us. Liam and Aidan. We're here to help you, to protect you."

He let go of his necklace of stones and clasped Aidan's hand in both of his. "I know you are, and I appreciate it."

The door from the bedroom opened, and Blake stepped out. He took one look at his husband and said, "Ricardo, you look terrible. Whatever you're talking about, it's enough. Come to bed."

"Yes, *mi amor*," Ricardo said meekly, and he followed Blake into the bedroom. The door shut sharply behind them.

8 – Threat Levels

Once the bedroom door closed behind Ricardo and Blake, Aidan stood up. "This is more serious than we thought," he said. "From what Ricardo said, there seems to be a real threat against him."

"Let's not jump to any assumptions yet," Liam said. "Of course, we've approached this operation as if the threats are real, and we're not going to change that. But we have no proof that these threats were real, only Ricardo's word. He's paranoid, and that business with the crystals does not inspire confidence in the clarity of his thinking."

"What do we do?"

"We keep on the way we've planned. When does Ricardo speak?"

"Not until Thursday morning. But he wants to attend most of the sessions."

"One of us will have to be with him at all times. Have you got a program for this conference?"

"I can pull it up online." Aidan got his laptop, hooked up to the hotel Wi-Fi, and navigated to the conference website. "There's a plenary session tomorrow at ten AM, a welcome by the organizers, introduction of the speakers and so on." He scanned through the list of events. "I had no idea there were significant populations of Jews in over two dozen countries in Central and South America and the Caribbean. It looks like the top ten will each get their own session, with one or more speakers, and then the rest of the area will be handled with panel discussions."

"This is the kind of thing you're interested in," Liam said. "You can sit with Ricardo when he wants to hear a speaker, and I'll be on him whenever we go out."

"What are you going to do while I'm with Ricardo?"

Liam grinned. "Work out? Swim? Hang out with your ex and get all the dirt about your relationship?"

"I like the first two suggestions better than the third. Besides, Blake will probably be busy working all the time."

They went into their bedroom a short while later. Aidan left the sliding glass door cracked, so that he could hear the waves outside. He slipped quickly into sleep, lulled by the repetitive sounds. When he woke the next morning, the door was wide open and Liam was on the balcony doing sun salutations in a tight-fitting pair of nylon shorts.

Aidan watched as Liam raised his hands, stretched and bent, eventually lying flat on the concrete balcony. Aidan doubted he would ever get tired of watching Liam work out, seeing the way his muscles flexed, the actions of that superb body that was his to explore in intimate moments.

They both showered and were dressed and waiting in the living room of the suite when the door to the other bedroom opened and Blake stepped out. He looked like he'd gotten some rest, which was good. At least one thing hadn't changed; on vacation, Blake still wore the same dress slacks and oxford-cloth button down shirts that he had all those years ago.

Ricardo stepped out behind him, in a well-tailored charcoal gray pinstripe suit that accommodated his broad shoulders. He looked exhausted, with dark circles beneath his eyes. *But it suits him*, Aidan thought. He resembled an El Greco Jesus, with his dark, curly hair and a handsome yet haunted look.

"What shall we do for breakfast?" Aidan asked, conscious that he'd eaten little the day before beyond some cinnamon rolls at the hotel in Philadelphia and then a couple of slices of pizza.

"I don't want to leave the room," Ricardo said. "You can do what you like."

Blake was once again laying out pills for Ricardo. Aidan wondered what they were—anti-psychotics? Mood enhancers? Or, more prosaically, for things like high blood pressure or cholesterol?

"There is a continental breakfast buffet before the opening session." Blake turned to Ricardo. "You have to show your face, love. Otherwise, what's the point of coming all this way if you're going to hide in the hotel room and never go to any of the sessions?"

Aidan was surprised to hear that endearment coming from his ex. Blake had always called him Aidan, or Aid, but never sweetheart, honey, or love.

"You are right, of course," Ricardo said. He smiled at Blake.

"You should tell Blake what you told us last night," Liam said. "About the threats you have been receiving."

"I know about them," Blake said. "At least the calls that came after Ricardo went to the hospital."

Ricardo turned to him. "You knew?"

"Of course. I answered your phone, remember? Why do you think

I agreed to hire you bodyguards for this conference?"

"It would have been nice of you to tell us before we got here," Aidan said to Blake. "Instead of letting us believe that this was all in Ricardo's head."

Aidan was surprised to see Blake look abashed, and even more that he apologized. "I'm sorry. I only took a couple of calls, and I wasn't sure how serious they were."

"Do you remember what the caller said?" Liam asked.

"Not exactly. He said that Ricardo should keep his mouth shut, and not come to this conference."

"But it was a man's voice?"

Blake nodded. "With some kind of accent."

"Spanish?"

"I don't think so. I want to say Middle Eastern, but I'm not sure." He turned to Aidan. "He had that kind of throat clearing noise when he pronounced his H's, the way you used to when you said Hebrew words."

"You've handled a lot of international clients, Blake," Aidan said. "Think. Was the accent Israeli? Arabic? Maybe Persian, because of the Iranian connection?"

Blake frowned. "He didn't say enough for me to get a clear idea. And I was frightened, so I wasn't thinking clearly."

"It's a good lead," Liam said. "If you're ready to go, Ricardo, I'll walk you and Aidan down to the breakfast and the opening session. Aidan can text me when you're finished, and I'll come back for you."

Ricardo agreed, and the three of them walked down the long

hallway to the elevator lobby. The first car that arrived was crowded, and though there was room for the three of them, Ricardo balked and they had to wait for an empty one.

Once downstairs, they passed the fountain with frolicking dolphins, and Ricardo paused again to dip his necklace of stones into it. "Why do you do that?" Liam asked.

"I'm blessing the waters," Ricardo said. "Sharing the healing energy of my crystals."

They'd had a lot of odd clients, Aidan thought, as they continued, and Ricardo was in the running for the oddest. How much of that came from all those pills?

It wasn't far from there to the convention center, and Liam left them at the door. Ricardo checked in at the registration desk and purchased a guest pass for Aidan, which would allow him to attend all the sessions.

They entered a big classroom-style room with a sloped floor and rows of tables with individual swiveling seats. Aidan expected Ricardo to hurry to a seat and stay there with his head down, but instead he recognized a man standing the entrance and hurried over to him, speaking in rapid Spanish. Aidan could only catch a few words, but it appeared they were catching up after not seeing each other for several years.

Ricardo was different, more animated, than Aidan had seen him before. It was as if he was finally able to relax once he was in the conference area.

Other men and women came over to join their conversation, and

Aidan lingered in the background. He wanted to get something to eat, but Ricardo was too busy talking, and Aidan couldn't leave him. He managed to grab a couple of small Danish pastries on their way to their seats.

Ricardo wanted to sit in the middle of the row, but Aidan directed him to a seat at the aisle, so that they could leave easily and quickly, presenting less of a target. But he felt uncomfortable there, as people went in and out the rear doors, and he texted Liam that he needed backup outside the conference room.

Liam didn't complain, simply texted back that he would be there.

Aidan found it hard to concentrate on the speakers, who either spoke in English or Spanish, with simultaneous translation through headphones, because he was so focused on the movement of people around the room. Every time the rear door opened, he stiffened.

He was relieved when the conference broke for lunch. His stomach was rumbling, and he was stressed. A pair of men Ricardo had spoken with earlier came over to invite him to lunch. He looked at Aidan. "Why don't you join your friends? Liam and I will follow you and sit near you in the restaurant, so we'll be around if you need us."

Ricardo agreed. He and the two men left the convention center, with Aidan a few feet behind them. When he spotted Liam, he explained the situation. "I'd like to choose where they eat and where they sit," Liam said.

"Let's see what they pick first," Aidan said.

One of the men clearly took the lead, and Ricardo and the other man followed him down the hallway. Halfway toward the next tower, they stopped at a restaurant run by a world-famous chef, featuring Mediterranean cuisine. "Oh, great, I wanted to try this place," Aidan said. "I've read about this chef online forever."

"It looks okay," Liam admitted. They watched as the three men approached the hostess and spoke with her, and then as she led them to a half-round table in the back of the restaurant.

"The man with Ricardo is sharp," Liam said. "I couldn't have picked a better table for them myself. Each one of them has a view of the whole room, with no chance anyone is at their back."

"They're all Latin diplomats," Aidan said. "Give them some credit for knowing about personal safety."

When the hostess returned, Liam asked for a table toward the back, and when they were shown to a four-top they sat across from one another, so Aidan could keep an eye on the client and Liam could face the front door.

Aidan relaxed for the first time that morning. Ricardo was in a safe situation, he and Liam were together, and the menu looked mouth-wateringly good. Aidan was in the mood for a salad, but why order that in a high-end restaurant? He opted for the butternut squash tortelli, while Liam ordered the burger, medium, with bacon and a barbeque aioli.

"What?" Liam said, after he ordered, when he saw the look on Aidan's face. "I judge a place by how well they can make a burger."

"I'll look forward to your critique, then," Aidan said drily.

Liam picked up his water and took a sip. "What's your take on the relationship between Blake and Ricardo?"

Aidan sat back in his chair. "Interesting. I've been trying to figure out what Ricardo and I have in common that could have attracted Blake to both of us."

"Besides the Jewish thing, you mean? You've said before that some WASPy guys get off on that."

"Yeah, I suppose. But we come from such different backgrounds and our approach to religion is very different. It sounds like Ricardo is way more observant than I am, for example. And he's Latin, while I'm white bread American."

"You're more handsome than Ricardo."

Aidan looked at him. "You're just saying that."

"It's true, I love you, so of course you're handsome to me. But he has a big nose and beetle brows. And he always looks like he ate something that disagreed with him."

"He's probably smarter than I am," Aidan said. "He has that job at the foreign policy institute. You need brains for that."

"Says my Ivy League graduate," Liam said. "You have a master's degree, like he does. If you wanted a more intellectual job, you could get one."

"Not at this point in my career," Aidan said. "Anyway, it's all water under the bridge, isn't it? He's with Blake and I'm with you, and I couldn't be happier."

After lunch, they followed Ricardo and the other two diplomats back to the convention center, where the three of them stopped in the lobby to talk to another group, including a couple of women academics. Aidan recognized them even in casual clothing—the hair up in buns, the funky glasses, the way they seemed ready to break out into a lecture at any moment.

Aidan and Liam repeated their positions of the morning, Aidan with Ricardo and Liam outside, watching the doors. The speakers that afternoon included one of the academic women, who spoke about the resurgence of the Jewish community in Brazil, which had begun with one of the country's earliest settlers, Gaspar da Gama, who fled Portugal's inquisition in the 1600s.

"The first Jewish place of worship in the Americas, Kahal Zur Israel Synagogue, was founded in Recife on the northeast coast of the country as early as 1636." She paused and looked up. "Portuguese Jews developed the earliest cultivation of sugar. Further groups settled in the Amazon to cultivate rubber, while at the start of the twentieth century Russian Jews settled in Rio Grande do Sul, Brazil's southernmost state. Today Brazil has the ninth-largest population of Jews, over 100,000."

She went on to discuss the challenges facing Brazilian Jews, including intermarriage and emigration to Israel. Aidan was intrigued by the material, and he could see that Ricardo was as well, though he had to already know most of it.

"One of the most important things about the Jewish community in Brazil is the way that anti-Semitism is explicitly prohibited under the constitution, as are all forms of racism and religious intolerance, including the manufacture and distribution of swastikas. In that way, Brazil is a model for religious tolerance throughout the world, and the Anti-Defamation League ranks Brazil among the least anti-Semitic countries in the world."

Having seen the rise of intolerance in the United States, from anti-Semitism to the resurgence of the Ku Klux Klan and other white supremacists, as well as the growing anti-Muslim sentiment roiling Europe, Aidan felt it was good to know there were places in the world like Brazil where the threat level was low.

9 – Trapped

Liam took up his post outside the door when the afternoon session began. His least favorite part of close protection was the endless waiting around outside hotel rooms and offices for clients to conduct their business. It was important to stay vigilant, and yet the work was so dull. It was so far to the outdoors, and he felt trapped by the weight of the entire complex around him.

He occupied himself by watching people as they came down the hallway past the convention center. Who was on vacation, who was there for business, who was local?

There were obviously other conferences going on at the hotel at the same time—Liam spotted a clutch of Chinese men and women in matching dark suits, a dark-skinned man in an African dashiki in intense conversation with a hefty man in a polo shirt with the name of a Nassau company on the breast, a group of twenty-something women carrying matching tote bags advertising a cosmetics brand.

The harried moms and dads, accompanied by small children in various states of clothing, from swim diapers to miniature hoodies and sagging shorts, were on vacation, though how much of a vacation could it be for them with babies crying and kids pouting?

All in all, he'd rather be in charge of one middle-aged man with obvious neuroses.

Which brought him back to Ricardo, and Blake. It was interesting seeing in the flesh the man he'd heard so much about over the years. Indeed, Blake was as buttoned-up and borderline rude as he'd expected from Aidan's comments.

But what surprised Liam was the genuine love Blake displayed for Ricardo. When they talked about threats, Blake's eyes were full of fear for his husband. When Ricardo was mulish or irritated, Blake was submissive, and when Ricardo was frightened Blake was gentle and loving.

Had he been that way with Aidan, too and Aidan had missed it? After all, Blake had moved heaven and earth to find out where Aidan had gone when he left Philadelphia, and had traveled all the way to Tunisia to bring him back.

Bring him back, he thought. Not woo him back. Indeed, his only previous interaction with Blake had been backing Aidan up at the doorway, chasing Blake away like Aidan was a prize the two of them were fighting over.

Liam hadn't felt that way at the time. Aidan had made it clear he preferred to stay with Liam in Tunis rather than return to Philadelphia with Blake, and Liam was there to support that decision. He still recalled Blake's face that day – showing irritation rather than the pain of lost love.

If anything happened to Ricardo, Liam was sure he'd see that kind of pain on Blake's face. It was up to him and Aidan to make sure that didn't happen.

He moved around every ten minutes or so, from the lobby of the convention center to the hallway outside, changing his perspective and keeping his attention sharp. He was surprised that there were no visible signs of security. Even the registration desk had shut down, so anyone could walk in or out of the auditorium without challenge.

Liam wasn't sure what he could do if someone suspicious showed up. He had no authority at the hotel or the convention center, and he had no relationship with the group that had organized the event. All he could do, he decided, was follow anyone suspicious into the auditorium and be prepared for danger.

Individuals went in and out, all of them wearing a name badge on a lanyard, either to use the restroom or head down the hall for coffee.

He was relieved when the session broke at four o'clock. He stood to the side as people streamed out, chattering in a multitude of languages. Aidan and Ricardo were among the last ones out.

"Good session?" Liam asked Ricardo as he stepped into pace beside them.

"There was little I didn't already know," Ricardo said. "But I'm not here to learn. I'm here to present my information. It will be up to the others to listen and learn."

Well, that was imperious, wasn't it? But he couldn't blame the man, if he had the information he said he did.

They walked slowly down the hallway, giving the crowd ahead of them time to besiege the elevators, and waited until they had a car to themselves. "When we get upstairs, can you show us the information you have about Iran's involvement in this bombing?" Liam asked.

"You don't trust me that it's real?"

"It's not that I don't trust you. I want to make an independent evaluation. Consider what will happen after you reveal this material. What kind of threat will you be under then?"

"I have already prepared a document outlining my speech, including the proof I have," Ricardo said. "It will be uploaded as part of the conference proceedings. There will no longer be a need to keep me quiet about it."

"I wouldn't be too sure about that," Liam said, as the elevator doors opened.

Through the open door to the second bedroom, Liam saw Blake there on the phone. "I will get my information for you," Ricardo said, and walked into the bedroom. He returned with the messenger bag he had carried on the plane. He opened it and pulled out a folder.

The first document was apparently an email, and though the characters were Arabic, Liam couldn't recognize any of the words. "What am I looking at?" he asked, as he and Aidan sat on the couch together.

"This is an email from a senior official in the Iranian government," Ricardo said, as he sat across from them. "His name is Cyrus Esfahani. The email is to a man named Dilshad Jahangir. If you turn the page, you will find the English translation."

With Aidan looking over his shoulder, Liam read the translation. It was unpolished, the grammar rough, but it appeared to authorize Jahangir to proceed with the operation they had discussed.

"Not very specific, is it?" Liam asked, when he finished.

"Continue to read."

Liam flipped through the pages, giving Aidan a chance to read.

Ricardo had documentation that placed Jahangir in Buenos Aires on the day of the attack. His fingerprints matched ones found at the scene, and someone had been able to get into Jahangir's bank account and find a transfer of a little over a billion Iranian rials from the account of an Iranian company.

"A billion rials?" Liam asked.

"About twenty-five thousand dollars at that time," Ricardo said.

"It's pretty incriminating evidence," Aidan said, when they had finished looking through everything. "What happened to Dilshad Jahangir?"

"He was never indicted," Ricardo said. "He died about ten years ago in prison in Tehran."

"And Cyrus Esfahani?"

"He is the current minister for national defense," Ricardo said. "In the middle of negotiating a deal with the P5+1 to stop Iran's nuclear research in exchange for the relaxation of trade sanctions."

"Who's the P5+1?" Liam asked.

"The five permanent members of the United Nations Security Council, plus Germany."

Liam sat back. The couch was too soft, and he didn't want to slip back into it, but his back hurt from standing so long that day, so he hunched forward again. "This information is going to look bad for Esfahani, and perhaps damage these negotiations. You're playing with fire here, Ricardo."

"I know the AMIA bombing was a terrible event, and it's important that the people behind it be brought to justice," Aidan said.

"But is there a greater good at stake here? If you damage the negotiations, does that mean Iran continues its nuclear program? What if they complete a bomb and decide to use it against Israel?"

"A man like Esfahani cannot be trusted," Ricardo said. "What I expect will happen is that he will be replaced, and the negotiations will continue."

"You can't be sure of that," Liam said. "You're risking your personal safety on something that could potentially boomerang and hurt many other people."

"It is already done," Ricardo said. "Even if don't give my speech on Wednesday, three months ago I gave this material to the conference organizers to be part of their printed proceedings."

Liam looked at Aidan. "Then it doesn't look like we have any other options other than to proceed as we have been." He turned his head at a slight sound and noticed Blake standing in the doorway of the bedroom. How much had he heard? Did it matter?

The awkward silence in the room carried on for several minutes. Finally, Blake said, "I think we need to do something to take our mind off these problems. There's a huge walk-through aquarium here, Ricardo. Would you like to go down and see it?"

He turned to Aidan and Liam. "Lately, Ricardo loves fish and lizards."

"I'm learning to speak to them," Ricardo said. "I can communicate well with dogs and cats, and some birds."

Here we go again, Liam thought. Ricardo had seemed so rational and logical only a few moments before. Now he'd jumped on the crazy train again.

"We have to go past the pet store at least once a week," Blake continued. "So Ricardo can commune with fish and bearded lizards."

"Not one for lizards myself," Liam said. "Saw too many of them in the desert. Maybe we ought to stay here."

Ricardo stood up. "No, Blake is right. If we stay here, I will worry more. And I would like to see the fish."

Aidan got out the map as they walked to the elevator. The aquarium was in the base of the Royal Towers, quite a hike from where they were, and Liam didn't like the idea of parading the client down endless corridors and through crowded lobbies. But one of his primary rules in dealing with clients was not to interfere with their desires or schedules unless there was a clear and present danger.

The halls were crowded with vacationing families—tiny kids clutching stuffed porpoises and sharks, girls with long wet hair and towels wrapped around their bodies, teen boys slouching behind parents, too cool to be seen with them.

There were so many people around that it would be simple for one of them to sidle up to Ricardo and stick a knife in him before either he or Aidan could react. But the day's conference had rejuvenated Ricardo, so if he wanted to go see some fish, they'd go.

Liam let Aidan and Ricardo lead the way, with Blake a few steps behind typing something into his phone. Aidan had been right that Blake was a workaholic; Liam hadn't yet seen the man relax, grab a fruity drink or bop along to the ever-present Caribbean music.

They reached a grand lobby with a curving marble staircase down to the ground level. They had to show their room keys to get past the elaborately garbed security guard. Even though the man looked foolish, he was large enough to prevent anyone who wasn't a guest from following them downstairs, and Liam was grateful for small mercies.

They descended the stairs. Ricardo was telling Aidan a story and waving his arms expansively, so Liam kept a close eye on him. It would be more than embarrassing to lose a client to a broken neck, and if Ricardo took a tumble, Liam didn't want him taking Aidan down, too.

When they reached the ground, they followed signs to an expansive wall of glass that looked into a huge aquarium. A nurse shark glided past a school of bright blue and yellow parrotfish, some with yellow tails, others with purple.

The ceiling was low, and the overall experience was as if they were in a cave beneath the water's surface, the walls of the aquarium designed to look like they'd been naturally hewn from rock. It was an impressive experience, more immersive than any aquarium Liam had visited as a schoolkid or an adult.

Ricardo took a step back from the windows as if he'd received an electric shock. "I can't," he said, then stumbled back toward the stairs. "They're in prison. They're in pain!"

Liam was right behind him. "It's all right, Ricardo." He put his arm around the big man's shoulders. "They're just fish."

"I can sense their pain." Ricardo shuddered and twisted under Liam's grasp. "I feel the same way. I'm trapped inside this mental illness and I'm dying here."

Liam looked back at Aidan. His partner was always the one who was better with emotions, but he was busy with Blake, who stared catatonically at Ricardo, his own shoulders shaking.

Liam put his arm around Ricardo's shoulders and guided him back to the staircase, speaking reassurances to him that he didn't know if he felt himself.

10 – Enjoy Ourselves

After the four of them climbed the stairs back to the main level, Blake left Aidan's side and walked over to take Ricardo's arm. Liam stayed on point, leaving Aidan to pick up the rear.

What had happened there? Before they went to the aquarium, Ricardo had said that he could communicate with fish and lizards, and Aidan had dismissed that comment as a minor part of the client's paranoia. Aidan didn't believe it was possible to talk to fish, though he knew that some species had an even greater brain to body weight ratio than humans.

It was frightening to watch the way Ricardo reacted as soon as he reached the aquarium. Something had definitely affected him. Could the medication he was taking make him especially susceptible to the emotions and conditions of others? Quite possibly. Who knew, after all, what the combined effect was of all those pills Blake put out for Ricardo each morning and night? Aidan wasn't willing to write Ricardo off as a complete lunatic.

He moved up closer behind Blake and Ricardo to overhear their conversation. "This is our vacation, Ricardo," Blake said firmly. "I understand you are upset by so many things going on, but you can't shut yourself up in our room and eat fast food when there are so many wonderful places to eat here. Can't we have a small chance to enjoy ourselves?"

Even though he'd been subjected to the same kind of

manipulation, Aidan was impressed at the way Blake was able to use his lawyerly skills to construct an argument that would be difficult for Ricardo to refuse.

"For you, I can eat," Ricardo said finally. "But it must be somewhere we can be safe."

Aidan stepped up then. "How about if we go out toward the marina?" he suggested. "There will be fewer crowds that way, and more open space. Last night when I went to pick up the pizza, I saw a bunch of small restaurants out there. A Caribbean place with music, a Chinese restaurant, a burger bar."

Ricardo agreed, and Aidan took over point from Liam to lead them outside as quickly as he could. Even though it was late afternoon, the sun was still bright, the shadows long over the pavement.

They walked down a long stone staircase to the marina level, where they were immediately confronted by a series of expensive yachts. Some were clearly occupied, with towels stretched over chairs and crew members cleaning up, while others, from ports as exotic as Tangier and Kuala Lumpur, looked like they had been docked for a long time.

"I'd love to be rich enough to own one of these yachts," Blake said, pointing at a long, sleek yacht with racing stripes painted on the side.

"People that wealthy have troubles of their own," Aidan said. "We had a client a couple of years ago who was one of the richest men in Germany, and he was so frightened people would come after him that he spent most of his time on his yacht, moored off the coast of Saint Tropez."

"Not a bad way to live," Blake said.

"It is if you're too scared to enjoy yourself," Liam said. "We had to protect him when he flew to a meeting in Venice. One of the most beautiful cities in the world, and he stayed cooped up in his hotel room the whole time."

He couldn't help comparing that situation to this one. Once again, they were in a gorgeous location, with a client too paranoid to enjoy it.

Aidan led the way around the curve of the marina. The Caribbean bar was too noisy, the burger joint too crowded. The Chinese restaurant was dim and quiet, and they were able to get a table in the back with a sweeping view of the boats and the tourists.

Ricardo perked up once they were seated, but by the time dinner was over he was almost catatonic, and the four of them hurried up to the suite, lucky to grab an empty elevator on the first try. Liam opened the door first, as per their routine. With all four of them gone, it was important to make sure there were no threats lurking in the suite. Aidan held Ricardo and Blake outside while Liam checked each bedroom and bathroom, then called out "Clear."

Liam went into the bathroom he shared with Aidan. "I am going to sleep," Ricardo said, and after a quick kiss on Blake's cheek he went into the other bedroom.

At least Blake hadn't changed his disdain for most forms of affectionate display. He still tolerated only the occasional kiss—never to his lips, only to his cheek or forehead.

Ricardo closed the bedroom door behind him, and Aidan opened the sliding door to the balcony. Fresh, warm air flooded in, with the distant sound of steel drums and children laughing.

Blake collapsed onto the sofa. It was clear that Ricardo's behavior had been wearing on him, even with Aidan and Liam there to help handle the load. "Can I ask you a question?" Aidan asked.

"Why not?"

"Why did you start following me on Facebook?"

Blake's face reddened a shade darker. "It was Ricardo's idea. He was interested in you. Reasonably, not in a stalker way. After all you and I were together for a long time and he was curious." He looked at Aidan. "Why did you accept my friend request?"

Aidan shrugged. "Like you said, we were together for a long time. I admit I was curious to dip into your life now and then. When you checked in to restaurants where we used to go together. That kind of thing."

"Ricardo was fascinated by all the different places you visited. Corsica, Turkey, New Jersey, Russia. He kept waiting for you to go to South America. 'There are a lot of people there who need protection,' he said, a couple of times."

"That's not likely to happen, because we stopped taking new clients a year ago, and switched our focus to corporate security."

"We saw that, and we were curious. Did something go wrong on a job?"

Aidan shook his head. "Not on an assignment. It was stupid, really. A big storm blew through the foothills of the Alps last year, and we had some damage to our roof. Liam climbed up a ladder to check it out, and he fell off and broke his arm. We both decided that we were getting too old for the physical part of close protection, so we stopped."

"Did that bother you?" Blake asked. "It's obvious that you and Liam work very well together."

"We still work together, just without as much danger." Aidan leaned back against the couch. "We're still evaluating the threat level here. If someone might follow through on those threats against Ricardo."

Liam came out of the bathroom then, his face wet and his hair damp. He sat beside Aidan on the sofa.

"What do you think?" Blake asked. "Should we get on a plane tomorrow and go back to Philadelphia?"

Aidan had been thinking along those lines, and he was interested to hear what Liam would say.

"I think Ricardo has put his cards on the table, and he needs to play the hand," Liam said. "The only way to remove this threat from him is to expose all that evidence."

"What about reprisal? There's nothing to stop this Esfahani from coming after him, or sending someone after him, is there?"

The gentle Caribbean beat outside shifted to harsh American rap music from the bandstand near the pool. "We don't know Esfahani or what his end game is," Liam said. "This bombing was what, almost twenty-five years ago? Who says the world will even care?"

"Liam," Aidan said indignantly. "People were killed. This was a terrorist attack by one country on the citizens of another."

"And that matters to you and to me, and to Ricardo," Liam said. "And it's possible the world at large will take note and there will be consequences for Esfahani. But it's also possible that nothing will happen."

"It mattered to Alberto Nisman," Aidan said. "I did some research once Ricardo told us about the information he has. Nisman was the prosecutor who investigated the bombings, and their link to Cristina Fernández de Kirchner. He was murdered shortly before he could unveil his proof. And now Kirchner and her henchmen are accused of covering up the very information Ricardo is about to make public."

"Then it's even more important that we stay vigilant." Liam looked at Blake. "Aidan and I have years of experience at keeping clients safe. And one of the most important things we tell clients is that sticking to a focus on daily life is best for the client. Leave the security to us."

Blake wasn't happy with that, but he agreed to stay on, and keep Ricardo at the conference.

"We probably should not have taken this assignment," Aidan said, when he and Liam were in their room together. "There's too much history between Blake and me. And Ricardo has been asking me questions about the time I spent with Blake. I'm not sure if he's curious or jealous."

Liam sat on the edge of the bed. "Come here," he said, and he patted the space next to him.

Aidan sat, and leaned his head against Liam's shoulder.

"Second-guessing ourselves now doesn't do anyone any good," Liam said. "We're here, and we need to make the best of it."

"I know." Aidan sighed. "And I'm over Blake, I know that. My life is so much more wonderful since I met you. But we spent nearly eleven years together, and it freaks me out to see echoes of that time creeping in."

"Do you want me to order you around?" Liam asked, and Aidan heard the rumble of a laugh coming through Liam's body.

"You already do that," Aidan said.

"You love it from me, though. For example, if I told you to take off all your clothes and lie on your back on the bed, you'd be happy to do it."

"Liam." Aidan elbowed him in the side.

"I'm not kidding, sailor. That's an order."

Liam stood up, leaving Aidan at a slight tilt on the bed. "Go on, get moving."

There was a glint in Liam's eye that Aidan knew well. He jumped up, pulling off his polo shirt as he did. He kicked off his deck shoes and unbuttoned his slacks at the same time, and then tugged the pants and his boxers down. He left them pooled on the floor and fall back on the bed, his legs spread.

Liam, meanwhile, remained fully clothed, though Aidan saw his husband's dick stiffening in his pants. It was a favorite game of Liam's, to keep Aidan naked and at his mercy while he stayed clothed, like an evil drill sergeant in a gay porn movie.

"Touch yourself," Liam commanded.

Aidan lay his palm flat on his stomach and looked up.

"That's not what I mean and you know it."

"I'm an English teacher," Aidan said. "I pay attention to words."

"Pay attention to this, then," Liam said, in his most commanding voice. "Wrap your hand around your dick and start to stroke it, or this little episode ends right now."

"You know just how to threaten me." Aidan followed Liam's instructions. His dick had begun oozing precome, and he used that to lube the movement of his hand. He looked up at Liam, and he was sure his eyes were already glazed with lust.

Liam moved around to the side of the bed and stuck his index finger toward Aidan's mouth. "Suck it."

Aidan complied, taking Liam's finger, rough from years of exercise, into his mouth and sucking on it. "Yeah, you want my cock in that mouth, don't you?"

"Yes, sir," Aidan said, speaking around the finger.

"Well, you're not going to get it." He pulled his finger out of Aidan's mouth. "Lift your legs."

Aidan complied, and Liam immediately stuck that wet finger into Aidan's ass up to the second knuckle. Aidan gulped but loved the feeling of having any part of Liam inside him. Liam began to push it forward, then pull it back, and Aidan had to catch his breath.

Liam was a man of many talents, so he was able to keep finger-fucking Aidan's ass with his right hand while he used his left to undo his pants and tug them down to his knees. Then he pulled his stiff dick out of the side of his jockstrap.

"Just get it wet," he commanded Aidan. "No sucking."

He shoved his dick at Aidan's face, and he swallowed it to the root, invoking his gag reflex. As he opened his mouth to gasp for air, Liam pulled out and then swung Aidan's legs around so he was sideways on the bed. He put one pillow under Aidan's head and another under his ass.

"I'm waiting here," Aidan said, between gasps. "Are you going to fuck me or not?"

"Pushy bottom." Liam moved close to Aidan's ass, held his dick to get the angle right, and then plunged in.

Aidan's mouth went dry and tiny electric shocks began shooting through his body. He looked up at Liam, looming over him, his polo shirt tight against his pecs and hanging loose at that perfect, smooth waist, grasped by the white waistband of the jock strap. What Aidan could see of his husband's thighs was skin stretched taut over muscles.

Liam gripped Aidan's waist so hard Aidan was sure there would be marks there the next day, but he didn't mind; he'd wear a brand on his forehead if that's what it took to keep Liam there.

Liam didn't care about such things, though he wasn't averse to teasing Aidan about the occasional handprint or hickey, proud of his possession. "You ready, baby?" Liam asked. "Cause I'm gonna come soon."

He released his right hand's grasp on Aidan's waist and began jerking Aidan in the rhythm of his thrusts. "Oh, Liam," Aidan panted. "Oh, yeah. Right there. My god. I'm gonna, I'm gonna…" and then he lost his words, so caught up in the rise of endorphins and the pressure shooting through his dick as if it was a fire hose.

Aidan squeezed his butt cheeks and Liam gasped, and then he shot off in his husband's ass.

"Love of my life," Liam said, leaning down to Aidan. He kissed him deeply. "*Amour de ma vie.*"

"My husband," Aidan responded. "Never going to get tired of saying that."

II – Migration

Aidan was happy the next morning because it looked like Ricardo had gotten a good night's sleep, and he was eager to get back to the conference. "A woman I correspond with, an expert on Jewish migration in and out of Latin America, is going to speak this morning," he said. "I am eager to hear her."

Even his attire said Ricardo was in a happier place—he wore a bright pink polo shirt and navy slacks, and the shirt reflected some color to his pallid cheeks. He was so eager to get to the convention center that Aidan had to scramble to keep up with him, dodging around teenagers intent on their phones and families with free-range little kids.

"I'm looking forward to this morning's sessions," Ricardo said as they ate miniature muffins and slices of fresh fruit from the buffet. "Ashley Goldstein-Wood and I have emailed in the past, though I have never met her."

They settled into their regular chairs, along the side walkway, as a young woman in a dark blue business suit with a white blouse took the stage. Aidan was amused to see that she also wore a blue-and-white polka dot bow in her hair. He hoped her speech would be as offbeat as her attire.

"My research focuses on the way that many Jews who landed in Latin America only stayed for a generation or two, before moving on to Israel or the United States," she began. "I am studying two questions. First, are those who head to the US doing so because their families were always set on the States, but were prevented due to immigration quotas? And second, why do those who leave for Israel do so? Are they moving toward greater religious connection, or away from persecution?"

It was an interesting question, in part because Aidan's situation was the opposite. His grandparents had been able to immigrate directly to the US, and yet he had moved to a life in France. It was good to know, though, that thanks to them he had his American citizenship, and could return home at any sign of trouble.

Provided that the US would still be safe for Jews, and people on the LGBT spectrum, for as long as he lived. Sometimes the news from home made him wonder about that.

He tuned back into the presentation. Professor Goldstein-Wood said that her grandparents had emigrated from Russia and Poland to Mexico when quotas prevented them from entering the US. Though her father and mother were both born in Mexico City and considered themselves Mexicans, they had sent her to study in Boston and she had chosen to marry an American and stay there. Only one of the cousins of her generation remained in Mexico.

Aidan liked the way that she twined her personal history with her research; it made her presentation come alive. Ricardo paid close attention and applauded heartily when she was finished.

The next presentation, though, seemed to upset Ricardo. The speaker was a representative of an aid agency that had launched an intensive public campaign to encourage Jews from Argentina and Uruguay to move to Israel and offered them extensive economic aid to help with their transition. He had done a dull study focused on statistics, and Aidan tuned out, focusing on the way that Ricardo's body tensed, how he leaned forward as if he was ready to interrupt the man or challenge his statistics.

By the end of the session, the social Ricardo had disappeared, replaced by the paranoid one. He insisted that he didn't want to go to lunch, nor did he want to attend the afternoon session. "I will work on my presentation for tomorrow," he said.

They met Liam outside the conference room and the three of them walked back to the room. Ricardo seemed particularly rabbity to Aidan, his attention constantly swerving from people passing by to a cleaning woman washing store windows to a bellman with a cart full of luggage.

"It's all right, Ricardo," Aidan said as they neared the elevator. "We'll be back in the room soon."

"But will I be safe even there?"

"Liam and I are here to protect you. You have nothing to worry about."

Ricardo pursed his lips and said nothing more. When they reached the suite, he went into the bedroom he shared with Blake. "Do you want anything for lunch?" Aidan asked Liam.

"I could go for a sandwich. Why doesn't Ricardo want to go back to the afternoon session?"

"He was good this morning, shaking hands, laughing, talking with people. He enjoyed his friend's presentation, but then he got tense during the next one. Maybe it's that, or perhaps this crazy business is all an act, and he's exhausted by it."

"I remember when I was still in the SEALs, and I had to pretend that I was straight. Sometimes it really wore me out."

Aidan was surprised by this unexpected revelation but couldn't pursue it because the door to the bedroom slammed open, and Blake strode out, carrying his laptop. "I'll be in the coffee shop on the ground floor," he said, and he was gone before Aidan could ask why he was upset.

Ricardo came out of the bedroom as soon as the door closed behind Blake. "Blake is angry that I will not go back to the conference," he said. "But I am too worried to concentrate."

His anxiety infected Liam, who strode around the living room. "Did something happen this morning? Something to trigger a fear?"

"I was fine during my friend Ashley's presentation, but when the next speaker came up I was bored and I turned on my phone." He shoved the phone at Aidan. "There are new threats."

As Aidan looked down, Liam stepped up close to him so they could both see. The first one read, "FORGET WHAT YOU KNOW" in capital letters.

Liam put his finger on the sender's email address. "We can get Robert to check this address out, can't we?"

Robert was a British hacker they had used in the past when they needed digital information. "He can try, but I bet you it won't go anywhere," Aidan said. "Look at the domain name."

"What's wrong with Filigre Diamonds?" Liam asked.

"Nothing, if whoever set up the domain could spell the name correctly. There are two e's in filigree." He pulled out his own phone and began typing. "The address filigrediamonds.com doesn't resolve to anything."

"How can they use it, then?" Ricardo asked.

"Lots of different ways," Aidan said. "But the simplest is to use an email anonymizer where you put in the username and domain you want to show up in the user's in-box. The anonymizer sends it from their own server and you never know it's spam."

"How do you know all that?" Liam asked.

"I pay attention when Robert talks," Aidan said dryly. "Let's see the next message."

Ricardo began pacing around the living room, but Aidan and Liam were too focused on the messages to try and calm him down. The next message came from a domain called cofeebeansinternational, this time missing an f in coffee. DO NOT GO TO BAHAMAS, in the same all-caps and font size.

"Well, we're getting closer," Aidan said. "Two misspelled words and a missing article. My guess is that these messages are coming from a non-English speaker. But if the person is Latinx, why not use Spanish?"

"Latinx?" Liam asked.

"Come on, Liam, keep up. Latinx is the non-gender-specific way of avoiding saying either Latina or Latino. My guess is Spanish because Ricardo is from Argentina."

"But we have articles in Spanish," Ricardo said. "*Los Bahamas.*"

"We're getting off target here," Liam said. "Someone wants you to forget what you know, and not come here to the Bahamas. Let's keep going."

The next read, "DIRTY JEW KEEP MOUTH SHUT OR DIE."

They quickly paged through the rest of the emails. "Did you report any of the earlier messages to anyone?" Liam asked.

Ricardo shook his head. "Who would I tell? The IT person at the Institute? The police?"

He began to shake, and Aidan put his arm around Ricardo. "It's all right. No one is going to harm you. Liam and I are here to protect you."

Aidan forwarded the threatening emails to Robert the hacker, then returned the phone to Ricardo. He knew that Liam would want to think about those phone threats, perhaps call Louis back in France and ask his opinion, which he couldn't do while he was in the room with them. "Liam, why don't you go for a swim? That'll relax you so you can be more vigilant if we go out later. Ricardo and I will stay here so he can work on his presentation. On your way back, you can pass by the deli, if you don't mind, and bring me back a sandwich."

Liam stared at him, and Aidan raised his eyebrows. It was as if all Liam's agitation passed out of him, and he said, "That's a great idea. Ricardo, you want anything?"

He waved his hand. "Whatever you bring for Aidan."

Liam went into the bedroom, and Aidan sat on the sofa. "There was a bit too much data this morning for me to process, but I got the gist of the meeting," he said to Ricardo. "The position of the Jews in Latin America is still precarious, right?"

Ricardo paused in his pacing. "Sometimes I believe we will only be safe if we all move to Israel and develop nuclear weapons to protect us from our neighbors."

Well, that was a darker approach than Aidan had gotten from what he'd heard, but Ricardo was paranoid, after all.

Liam came out of the bedroom wearing a T-shirt that Aidan had packed for himself, which displayed the words "Côte d'Azur" in a rainbow of colors, above an image of the pebbled beach at Nice. His black boxer trunks clung to his thighs, and he had a pair of dark green flip-flops on his feet. "I'll be back in a while. I have my phone, and I took the room card to pay for lunch."

After Liam left, Ricardo sat on the sofa across from Aidan. "You grew up in America, of course," he said. "You will not have felt any danger being Jewish."

"I grew up in Trenton, and then I spent years in Philadelphia, at Penn and then with Blake. I studied the Holocaust in Sunday school, and sometimes it was clear that I was in a religious minority, but no, I never felt danger because of my religion. Did you feel danger in Argentina?"

Ricardo nodded. "One of the first things we studied in Hebrew school was the Inquisitions in Mexico, in Central America, in what is now Colombia. The Peruvian Inquisition, headquartered in Lima, was responsible for administering Spanish territories in Panama and South America."

Aidan had learned little about the Jews of South America in Hebrew and Sunday school, and he was curious. "I didn't realize that the Inquisition had taken place outside of Spain and Portugal," he admitted. "But it makes sense."

"My father's family has been in Argentina for centuries. They left Spain in 1492, lived in France for a few hundred years, then came to Argentina in the early eighteen hundreds. I have traced my lineage on my father's side back to an ancestor called Henri Levy, who immigrated to Buenos Aires in 1815."

Ricardo picked up a pen from the table next to him and toyed with it. "Have you heard of Baron Maurice de Hirsch?"

"Another ancestor of yours?"

Ricardo shook his head. "He was a French Jewish philanthropist, who founded the Jewish Colonization Association. He believed that since Jews were farmers in Eastern Europe, they could thrive as farmers in the New World as well. His association paid the way for Jews to come from all over Europe and settle everywhere from the egg farms of Connecticut to the *llano* of Argentina. My mother's family left the *shtetls* of Russian and Poland for the promise of these open lands where they could be free to worship."

"My great-grandparents made the same journey," Aidan said. "Though they left later in the 19th century and came to the United States and settled in cities."

"My family gave up their farms as quickly as they could, moved to the city and became traders," Ricardo said. "It was my father's fondest wish that I get an education and become a doctor, a lawyer or a diplomat."

"The same dreams of Jewish parents all over the world," Aidan said. "Though in the past I'd have added rabbi to that list."

"I have several cousins in the rabbinate, in Argentina and in Israel."

Ricardo pulled out the tangle of necklaces from beneath his shirt. "They would not approve of my belief in the healing power of these stones, though some Orthodox rabbis do. You know the Orthodox world is generally divided between Modern Orthodox and Haredi, or ultra-Orthodox, right?"

"I've heard about the Haredi, but I haven't paid much attention to them. I assume they're the ones who don't believe in crystals?"

Ricardo nodded. "Or yoga, or reiki, or anything else we might consider New Age. But for me, I believe." He lifted a rope necklace over his head and laid it on the table. "This stone is clear quartz. They call it the master healer, and it resonates with the higher chakras, bringing in divine white light that heals emotional or physical problems."

Aidan nodded along. He knew a little about crystals, and that many people believed in their healing powers. But was Ricardo looking at them rationally, or was this another manifestation of his mental illness? Could any of these bring him back to the man he had been before his psychotic break?

And could any of those stones protect them from the threats that might have stretched from Argentina here to the Bahamas?

12 – Many Who Search

As soon as Liam left the suite, he considered where he could make a private phone call. He could have called from the second bedroom, but he was worried that even if he spoke quietly Ricardo might have overheard something, and he didn't want to worry the client unnecessarily.

When he got down to the lobby, there were people everywhere, waiting in line to register, clogging the hallways, even milling around outside. Finally he found a park bench under a palm tree, with his back to a steep decline that led to the street, so it would be hard for anyone to creep up behind him. He had a broad hundred-and-eighty-degree view, and there was no one close enough to overhear his call.

Nice was six hours ahead of them, so he felt comfortable dialing Louis's number. "How's the vacation going?" Louis asked, when he answered.

"Not quite a vacation." Liam told Louis about the series of phone and email threats Ricardo had received. "I'm worried that if they can't get at Ricardo directly, whoever is after him might threaten the conference. Any way you can dip into a channel somewhere and see if there have been any threats?"

"I never had much to do with the Caribbean, and the contacts I've had in the past who might know something are getting rustier. But I'll see."

Liam thanked him and hung up. Then he found an Olympic-sized swimming pool at one of the other towers, and was delighted to see they had lined up several lanes for speed swimmers. He showed his key card at the towel counter, a faux Bahamian hut with a straw roof, and signed the register with his name and room number.

He staked out a recliner and left his towel and T-shirt there. He had a waterproof pouch for his phone, which he clipped onto his shorts. Then he dove into an empty lane and began to swim the way he'd been trained, staying underwater each lap, only surfacing to breathe at the end of the pool before turning back around. He did ten laps that way, feeling his muscles stretch and flex, the endorphins of a good workout rising.

Then he moved over to a quiet area and began his regular workout—a hundred sit-ups, a hundred pushups, fifty jumping jacks, a dozen sun salutations. By then he was hot and sweaty, and he dove back into the pool for another ten laps.

As he stepped out of the water and reached for his towel, he noticed a man staring at him from a couple of lounges away. He was accustomed to attracting attention, particularly when he was nearly naked, and it didn't bother him. If other men wanted to stare at his body, they were welcome to. He could handle any unwanted advances, if they were made.

When the man stood up and walked over, he surprised Liam by asking, "Were you a SEAL?"

Liam looked more closely at the man beside him. He was about ten years younger, lean and fit in a way that said military training. "How could you tell?" Liam asked, as he dried his hair.

"The stroke. When I was in the Navy, we worked a couple of operations with a SEAL team, and they all swam in that combination of breast-stroke and freestyle. I was amazed at how long they could stay underwater."

Liam draped the towel over the back of the lounger, and reached out to shake the other man's hand. "Liam McCullough."

"Ryan Wood. You on vacation here?"

Liam shook his head. "Work. Client here for a conference."

"The Jews of Latin America?"

Liam looked at him closely. He had close-cropped blond hair a couple of shades lighter than Liam's own. Aquiline nose, square jaw. Didn't look Jewish at all—but then, he didn't have the same kind of Jewish radar that Aidan had.

"What makes you say that?" Liam asked.

"My wife's here for that. Ashley Goldstein-Wood. She's a professor of Judaic studies at Brandeis, outside Boston. Jews of Latin America are her thing."

Liam nodded. "Yeah, here for the same conference. You'll forgive me if I don't reveal any details about my client." He hesitated. He didn't like to involve outsiders in his assignments, but it could be useful to be in contact with someone like Ryan, who had a military background and whose wife was in the same field as Ricardo. "I'd like to keep in touch, though."

"Sure. You have your phone?" Ryan said.

They exchanged numbers, and then Ryan returned to his lounge, and Liam stretched out to bake in the sun. When he and Aidan first moved to Nice from Tunisia, they had lived only a few blocks from the Mediterranean, and Liam swam in the sea often. Now that they lived up in the hills, it was a luxury for him to find a place he could swim the way he wanted to, lap after lap, giving his muscles the workout they deserved.

He dozed off for fifteen minutes or so, his military instinct to grab a catnap whenever possible kicking in. He realized he wasn't wearing sunscreen, so he decided to call it quits, grab the sandwiches Aidan wanted and return to the suite.

He knew that Aidan would want a BLT, and he got one for himself as well, but wasn't sure if Ricardo could eat pork, so he got him a turkey sub sandwich. Three sodas and three bags of chips completed the order, and he carried the bag upstairs, the sodas cold against his bare leg.

In the suite, he found Aidan and Ricardo talking about crystals. Ricardo had a purple stone on silver chain on the table in front of him. "Amethyst provides clarity when there's confusion in the mind, and helps to relieve stress and anxiety." Ricardo smiled faintly. "I can certainly use that."

Liam joined the two of them at the table. He didn't want to interrupt what Ricardo was doing, so he left the sandwiches and sodas in the bag.

The next chain Ricardo tried to remove from around his neck was tangled with two others, and Aidan got up and went around behind Ricardo to unhook them. It was an oddly intimate moment, and Liam was surprised to feel a tiny bit of jealousy.

When Aidan had the three chains laid out on the table, he returned to his seat. "This pink stone is rose quartz," Ricardo said. "It's soothing and calming and good for emotional traumas. This yellow stone is citrine, and it protects your auras. And this is black tourmaline, which you can place near your electronic devices and gadgets to protect you from EMF frequencies."

Liam held up the bag. "Shall we eat lunch?"

Ricardo moved his stones and chains to one side, and Liam laid out the food. Ricardo ate without thanking Liam or seeming to appreciate what went into his mouth. As soon as he finished, he pushed aside the sandwich wrapping and the empty chip bag and pulled his stones over to him again, fingering them one by one and murmuring in a low voice.

The door to the suite opened and Blake came in, carrying his briefcase. "You're not obsessing over those stones again, are you?" he asked Ricardo.

"It is not an obsession," Ricardo said. "These stones heal me, and they direct me in my search for the missing god."

He turned to Aidan and Liam. "I have five of the six crystals I need to point me in the direction of the missing god," he said, in a tone so conversational that Liam could almost ignore the fact that the words made no sense.

"The missing god?" Aidan asked.

"There are twelve gods who rule the world, but the twelfth one is missing," Ricardo said. "We cannot put the world back in balance until the missing god is found."

"And you're in charge of that?"

"I am but one of many who search," Ricardo said. "Which reminds me. There is a crystal shop in Nassau I would like to visit. Can we go now?"

"You're not going back to the afternoon session?" Liam asked.

Ricardo shook his head. "The crystals tell me not to. They were vibrating in a way that made me uncomfortable."

"We can't have that," Liam said, trying to hide the sarcasm in his voice. "Then let's go to Nassau."

"Really, Ricardo?" Blake asked. "You came all this way for this conference, and now you want to skip out and go shopping?"

"I have to find my own way," Ricardo said, in a voice that was at once serene but also severe. Blake frowned, but he relented.

Ricardo put his crystals back on and insisted on carrying his messenger bag over his shoulder. The four of them rode down to the lobby and walked out to the driveway, where there was a long line for taxis. "I cannot wait around here," Ricardo said. "I have to go."

"There's a shuttle boat that goes over to Nassau," Aidan said. "The dock is across the street from the shopping center where we ate dinner last night."

"Lead the way," Liam said. Aidan took off with Blake beside him and Liam followed with Ricardo.

They walked down the long, winding driveway to the four-lane highway, and Aidan pointed ahead. They waited for a break in traffic to cross over to the ferry terminal, and even though they scurried a tourist bus nearly ran them down.

Tiny storefronts lined the walkway from the street to the ferry dock, selling everything from bottled water to decorated coconuts to T-shirts. Liam liked the one with the Warner Brothers WB logo and the words, "If you see da police warn a brother."

Blake bought them round-trip tickets and they walked out onto the dock to wait for the next ferry. A cool breeze swept in off the water as they surveyed the skyline of Nassau across the bay. A cluster of low buildings along the waterfront, with a few hotels off to the side. The water was a chilly blue green, and a cluster of low-rise apartment buildings painted in an array of pastel colors sat along the shore across from them.

While they waited, Liam pulled Aidan aside. "I called Louis and asked him to see if there have been any threats made against the conference."

"And I forwarded the emails to Robert to see if he can get any information from them." Aidan looked at him. "I wish both Blake and Ricardo had been more honest from the start about these threats."

"It is what it is," Liam said. "At least we know now."

"Is there anything we should be doing differently?"

Liam shook his head. "We walked into this job believing there was a credible threat, even before we saw the evidence, because that's the way we approach every assignment. All we can do is stay vigilant, protect the client. I'm happy we got him away from the hotel for a while. I didn't see anyone following us here, and once we get to Nassau we should be able to blend into the tourist traffic."

"Blake and Ricardo aren't exactly dressed like tourists."

"Yeah, but there are enough conventioneers on this island who are dressed more formally." He smiled at Aidan. "I know you're worried, sweetheart. But we're good."

The taxi, a low boat with a blue roof and white trim, pulled up and a group of European and American tourists got out. Then a young Bahamian man took their tickets and helped them onto the boat. None of their fellow passengers appeared to pose a threat—two middle-aged ladies with an elderly woman, probably their mother. A young couple in their twenties who couldn't keep their hands off each other – mostly likely on their honeymoon. And an older couple in matching floppy hats to protect their skin from the sun.

An older man with dark skin and a heavy accent acted as tour guide, pointing out the homes of the rich and famous along the shore, but the sound of the engine was so loud that Liam missed half of the narrative.

Ricardo listened intently, though, leaning forward, his attention on the man. What a curious guy, Liam thought. How much of what they saw was Ricardo's real personality, and how much the result of all those pills Blake gave him?

They docked in Nassau and climbed out of the boat, then up a level to the street. "I have the address of the shop on my phone," Ricardo said.

Ricardo pulled up the note he had left for himself with the address of the crystal shop, a few blocks inland. Liam used his own phone to get a map of the island and locate the shop, and then led the way.

He hoped that Ricardo would be calmed by the vibrations in the crystal shop, and that he would find what he was searching for. Anything that put a client in good spirits made it easier to protect him.

13 – Real World Problems

The crystal shop was a small storefront, the dusty front window plastered with boasts of what the crystals could do for clients. IMPROVE YOUR SEX LIFE, BRING PEACE AND SERENITY, and TUNE YOUR CHAKRAS. Aidan wasn't sure what a chakra was or why it needed tuning, but the first two could certainly be useful.

Aidan went inside with Ricardo and Blake, while Liam remained on the street. The store was filled with stones of all different colors and sizes, on tables, shelves and counters, in boxes and on display. An incense burner filled the air with a spicy scent over the industrial cool of the air conditioning, and Peruvian flute music played in the background.

The man behind the counter was rail-thin, with shoulder-length black hair in cornrows. "Good afternoon," he said in the kind of lilting accent that said 'vacation' to Aidan. "How can I help you?"

"Just looking." Ricardo moved quickly from one pile of stones to another, reading about their properties, picking one up here and there, hefting it in his hand, sniffing it with his eyes closed.

Blake stood by the door, a bored expression on his face, his arms clasped around his stomach. Could he be any less supportive? But then Aidan realized that all those stones around Ricardo's neck had come from stores like this, and perhaps Blake was being as nice as he could be.

Ricardo picked up a light orange stone. "Carnelian," he said to

Aidan. "You should consider this one. It will give you the perseverance you need to keep going in any tough situation."

Aidan took it from him. It was about the size and shape of a quarter, with a smooth surface. He held it in his hand, trying to feel vibrations, but got nothing. "Maybe another," he said, and put it back on the display.

The only other customers in the store were a mother and daughter, both with matching blonde cornrows. The mother was fascinated by the stones, showing some to her daughter, who was more interested in the display of reggae music CDs.

Aidan looked out the dusty window and saw Liam leaning back against the storefront, his head moving slowly from side to side as he assessed the street. Aidan picked up a piece of black obsidian that was supposed to protect from "fixation, sorcery and ill fortune." He thought Ricardo could use some protection from ill fortune, but when he read further he discovered it was a popular stone for witches and sorcerers, and could break curses, hexes, and spirit attachments.

He put the stone back down. Ricardo's problems were rooted in the real world, and while Aidan didn't dispute that some people could be helped by crystals, it would take vigilance and perhaps action to protect him, rather than the powers of a stone.

The mother bought a couple of stones and a velvet bag to carry them, and when she offered to buy her daughter a CD, the girl said she'd stream the music. The proprietor's eyes darkened, and Aidan hoped for the girl's sake that he wasn't one of the witches or shamans who used stones for evil.

Ricardo completed one circuit of the store. "There's nothing here I need," he said, and headed for the door.

"Thank god," Blake muttered to Aidan. "This crystal nonsense is getting out of hand. He has at least a dozen more of those rocks at home."

"If they make him more comfortable," Aidan said, but Blake snorted.

That was the Blake Aidan had known back in Philadelphia. It was strangely comforting to see the man he'd known hadn't completely disappeared.

As they walked outside, a pulse of traffic moved past them on the street, a half dozen taxis, a mix of local cars and trucks, and a sight-seeing bus blasting the song "I shot the sheriff."

"I am ready to return to the hotel," Ricardo announced.

"Why don't we stay here in Nassau for a while?" Aidan asked. "We're anonymous here. We can do some shopping, maybe have some lunch."

Ricardo shook his head. "No. I want to go back to the hotel right now." His tone was a mix of fear and spoiled child. A warm breeze swept along the street, swaying the fronds of the single palm tree on the sidewalk and shuffling some tourist debris forward—a fast food wrapper and an empty paper cup. It was humid and Aidan was starting to sweat.

Aidan smiled tightly. "Then it's back to the ferry dock."

Ricardo began to shake, and Blake put his arm around him. "It's all right, love. No one is going to harm you."

"No. A taxi." Ricardo stepped into the street and waved his arm at the oncoming traffic. Aidan had to grab his arm to keep him from walking directly in front of a low-riding car, its speakers blasting a song that was a combination of reggae and rap, with incendiary lyrics about fire and destruction.

Aidan shivered. It was important to remember they were in a foreign country with different cultures and standards. Despite the Bahamas' good-time reputation for tourists, the paperwork Louis had given them had spelled out the many ways a vacation could be ruined by theft or violence.

Surprisingly, a bright yellow taxi swerved out of the oncoming traffic, and Ricardo got into the front seat, leaving Blake, Liam and Aidan to squeeze into the back.

"Welcome to the Bahamas," the taxi driver said in a lilting accent. "Are you Christian men? I can recommend you to my church. Best in the islands."

"Atlantis Hotel," Blake said from the back seat.

"The pope will be replaced soon," Ricardo said, as the driver darted back into the traffic, squeezing into slot between trucks barely big enough for a scooter. "He is not able to bring the people together the way they need. The new pope will be a woman."

"A woman?" the driver asked.

"An Italian nun called *Soeur* Cristina," Ricardo said. "She won the Voice Italy competition a few years ago, and the pope has been grooming her to take over."

Aidan sat back and tuned out the conversation between Ricardo and the driver. There was only so much nuttiness he could take at once, and he wanted to think through everything that had happened that day. The way Ricardo had been so normal in the morning, then switched into paranoid mode. Ricardo's insistence on visiting the crystal store, then his quick determination to return to the hotel.

The revelation that Ricardo had new threats on his phone.

Aidan wanted to talk to Liam, but Blake was between them, and the cab wasn't the place for a solid conversation. The taxi drove through an area of run-down single-story houses painted in fading colors of pink and orange, where the yards were made of crushed rock and palm trees were few. It didn't seem like the same way the taxi had taken them from the airport.

He leaned forward. "Are you sure this is the way to Paradise Island?"

"Yah, mon," the driver said. "This special short cut I know. Bridge up ahead."

Aidan wasn't reassured, though, until he saw the signs for the toll road and the two curving spans, one heading to the island and the other back from it. As they climbed the bridge, a freighter passed heading out to sea, and to right he saw three big cruise ships docked. To the left were the high pink towers of Atlantis rising from the flat green land. The water was a dark blue, and Aidan wondered what hid beneath the sharp-edged waves.

This driver dropped them at the correct tower, and they spilled out in the driveway, reminding Aidan of clowns coming out of a car at the circus. Blake paid the driver and tipped him well, and they walked inside, Ricardo striding through the lobby with Liam hard on his heels.

Even though they'd been through a lot that day, the laid-back vacation feel of the lobby and the corridors made Aidan more relaxed. He spotted a security guard in a white uniform, and a family fresh from the dolphin encounter, the little boy clutching a stuffed dolphin like it was his new best friend.

Things would be fine, Aidan told himself. They were in a beautiful resort, surrounded by attentive staff and security. Ricardo would give his presentation and they'd head out. Mission accomplished, client safe.

As they passed the entrance to the conference center, a young, bearded man in a dark hoodie stepped toward them. "Mr. Levy?" he asked.

Liam immediately stepped between Ricardo and the man. "Who are you?" Liam asked.

"Ethan Silverberg," he said. "I run a blog on Jewish issues in Latin America."

Ricardo stepped around Liam. "Yes, I have read your blog," he said. "You do very well for someone without academic credentials."

Aidan had to repress a laugh.

"Yes, my credentials are in journalism, not in academic research," Silverberg said. When the man reached out to shake Ricardo's hand, his hoodie swung aside and Aidan saw his conference pass on a lanyard around his neck.

Ricardo spoke with him for a few minutes, and Aidan saw Liam was impatient to get moving again. Leaving the client exposed in the middle of the hallway, talking with a stranger, was against their standard protocols.

Finally, Silverberg reached his hand out to Ricardo again. "Thanks for talking with me. I'm looking forward to your presentation on Thursday."

When Silverberg walked away, Liam led them onward down the hallway, to the elevator. As he'd done before, Liam went into the suite first, leaving Ricardo, Blake and Aidan in the hallway. "I want to go inside," Ricardo insisted, after a long moment had passed.

"Give Liam time to make sure everything is safe." Aidan put his hand on Ricardo's shoulder to hold him back.

It took another minute or two before Liam opened the door to the suite wide. "Houston, we have a problem," he said. Aidan looked past him and saw that someone had been inside.

And torn the place apart.

14 – Motivations

Liam stared at the living room of the suite. The sofa pillows were on the floor, the fake hibiscus stems had been scattered and vase that held them turned upside down. The drawers of the desk had been emptied on the floor, the placemats from the table flung around the room. The small blue bag where Blake kept Ricardo's pills had been emptied, and vials were scattered on the table.

"What the hell happened here?" Blake demanded as he muscled into the room, with a lack of insight that did not surprise Liam at all.

"Looks like someone tossed the place." Liam turned to Ricardo, who stood there with his mouth agape, messenger bag still slung over his shoulder. "What were they looking for? What's in that bag you're carrying that's important enough for someone to break in here to search for it?"

"It is the proof I have of the Iranian involvement in the AMIA bombing."

"Blake, do me a favor?" Aidan asked.

"What? I'm not paying for any damages."

"Please check Ricardo's pills and make sure no one has messed with them."

Blake still looked clueless. "His pills?"

Liam watched Ricardo settle onto the sofa in a near-catatonic state. At least he wasn't freaking out, though Liam thought that was a possibility.

Aidan pulled Blake aside and spoke in a low voice, though Liam could hear their conversation. "We have to take every precaution. Make sure no one replaced a set of Ricardo's pills with something else, something toxic. You can pull up the Physician's Desk Reference on your laptop and check to make sure the pills are what he was prescribed."

"You think someone could do that?"

"I do. And you're the one who gives him his pills, so if he dies and an autopsy report shows he was given an overdose of sedatives, for example, the police will look at you."

Blake's eyes and mouth opened in horror. "When did you start thinking like that?"

"Sometime after you pushed me into a new life."

It embarrassed Liam how pleased he was to hear Aidan speak that way to Blake.

"Before you do that," Aidan continued, "you should run a virus scan. Your laptop was here when the intruder was."

"I can do that. I have a strong program my firm pays a lot of money for." Blake sat at the table with his laptop and Ricardo's pill bottles. Liam called the hotel desk and asked them to send someone from security up to the suite.

Aidan sat with Ricardo, who had begun to shake again, and tried to calm him. Liam walked into the bedroom that Ricardo and Blake shared, where the situation was the same. The bed had been stripped, the mattress turned on its side. The bureau drawers had been dumped on the floor, the clothes from the closet tossed as well.

Liam checked the phone, unscrewing the base with a screwdriver he kept on his keychain. It didn't look like anyone had messed with the phone, or installed any listening devices. He walked back out to the living room. "Blake. You might want to clean up some of the mess in there."

"That's what housekeeping is for."

"I meant, pick up your clothes," Liam said. "The maid won't know where you want things."

Blake closed the laptop. "All the pills are correct," he said. Then he got up and walked into the bedroom, while Liam checked out the room he had been sharing with Aidan. The scene was the same there, and as he moved around he hung shirts and slacks up in the closet and put underwear in drawers, though not as neatly as Aidan would have done.

He paid particular attention to the bags that had been stowed on the floor of the closet. Everything had been dumped out, which annoyed Liam more than anything. How was he supposed to check for anything missing when it was all so disordered?

It took him only a moment to realize how spoiled he was. Just because Aidan took care of the packing didn't mean Liam didn't know what they'd brought. He began packing the bags up the way he'd taught Aidan, noting when anything was missing. By the time he was finished he had a mental checklist, and he wasn't happy.

When he went back to the living room of the suite, Blake was yelling at a guard in a fancy white uniform with red epaulets. The guard clearly was not in charge, and the poor guy kept repeating to Blake that he had already called his supervisor, who was on his way.

While they waited, Liam called Aidan over. Blake gave up and sat on the sofa with Ricardo while the uniformed guard stood ineffectually by the front door. "Was any of our stuff taken?" Aidan asked in a low voice.

Liam nodded. "This was a very directed search, presumably for the paperwork Ricardo is carrying with him. But our searcher is an opportunist, too. He walked off with our two-way radios, which will keep us from maintaining contact if we split up. Both our pocketknives, which were the only weapons we have here. And our emergency medical kit."

"Why do that?" Aidan asked.

"So that if this person, whoever he or she is, attacks Ricardo we won't be able to save him."

Aidan looked stunned and rubbed his upper arms, where hairs had risen. "There's something I don't get," Aidan said. "If this person is after Ricardo, why not try to kill him back in the States, where it's a lot easier to get hold of a gun? Why all the threats?"

"You're the one who likes to spin out stories," Liam said. "Give me a scenario."

While Aidan thought, Liam heard Blake murmuring to Ricardo in the background. The door to the suite was still open; two maids moved down the hallway while speaking to each other, with the clank of one of the carts.

"Here's an idea," Aidan began, keeping his voice low. "Our guy—and I'll use the male term until we know otherwise—isn't a hired killer. Otherwise, like you said, he'd have tried to shoot or run over Ricardo back in Philadelphia."

Liam nodded. "Go on."

"His endgame is keeping Ricardo from releasing the proof he has. He does that, the threats stop. But Ricardo isn't playing along, so our guy has to come up with something else. We know now that he's here in Paradise Island, and he's getting more desperate. He broke in here to find that proof Ricardo has, but Ricardo's carrying it with him."

"Who do you think he is?" Liam asked.

Aidan pursed his lips and thought. "He's got to have a personal stake in this. Could he be the bomber?"

Liam shook his head. "Dilshad Jahangir? According to Ricardo, he died in prison in Tehran ten years ago."

"I'll get Robert to research Jahangir. See if he has any living relatives who want to keep his name out of this."

"Good. Beyond that, who's still going to care if this information comes out?"

"The Iranian government," Aidan said quickly. "Even though this happened years ago, they can't be happy about being accused of a terrorist act in a foreign country."

There was a brief rap on the door to the suite and the supervisor stepped in, a portly black man in a short-sleeved polo shirt with the resort logo on the breast. He wore a tag that said his name was Shadrach and that he was from New Providence. Liam led him into the bedroom he was sharing with Aidan and ran through the situation.

"Mr. Levy is here to speak at the conference on Jews in Latin

America. He received some threats back in the States, so he hired my partner and me to look after him while he's here."

"What kind of threats?" Shadrach had a tablet computer with him, and he began to take notes. First about the background situation, and then about that day in particular.

What time had they left the hotel? Had they told anyone they were leaving? Did they know anyone else at staying at the hotel?

"Mr. Levy knows many of the other speakers and attendees," Liam said. "The only person I know here is a man I met this afternoon, a former U.S. military man whose wife is a speaker at the conference." He gave Shadrach Ryan Wood's name and phone number.

Shadrach took note of the items the burglar had walked off with, and then called housekeeping to have someone come and clear the room. "You'll probably want to leave while the housekeepers are here," he said. "They'll have a lot of work to do."

"I'll see if I can convince Mr. Levy to leave. He's understandably very upset."

Shadrach shook his head. "This is not the kind of thing that happens here," he said. "We run a very safe property."

He left a few minutes later, after walking through all three rooms himself, and took the uniformed guard with him.

Aidan walked over to Liam and led him into their bedroom. "As I went to email Robert, I saw a new message from him. No luck on the threats I asked him to research. It looks like I was right, that the sender used an email anonymizer."

He handed the phone to Liam to read. Robert had tracked the

phone number the voicemail threats had come from, which was a beater phone available for purchase at any electronics store. He suggested that Ricardo install an app on his phone that would allow him to trap any future calls, even if they were from blocked numbers.

Aidan replied to Robert with thanks, and with the information he had on Cyrus Esfahani and Dilshad Jahangir. Liam watched as he typed, "Please send anything you can find on either of them, including surviving associates and family members."

They went back into the living room, and the four of them sat, two by two facing each other. "I need to install an app on your phone, Ricardo," Aidan said.

While Aidan took Ricardo's phone and downloaded the app Robert had suggested, Liam leaned forward and said, "Aidan and I have been speculating about who is behind these threats against you."

"It must be Cyrus Esfahani," Ricardo said, his arms crossed in front of him. "He is the only one still alive who could be hurt by these revelations."

"I've got our computer associate doing research on both Esfahani and Dilshad Jahangir," Aidan said. "For example, in case Jahangir has a son or daughter who wants to protect the family name."

"It has to be the Iranian government," Blake said. "They're negotiating a nuclear disarmament deal right now, in exchange for the relaxation of sanctions against them." He turned to Ricardo. "Wouldn't a revelation like this damage their credibility and endanger this agreement?"

Spoken like a lawyer, Liam thought. But Blake was right. Revenge was a strong motive, and so was protecting a family name, but foreign trade was even stronger. "Ricardo, can you help us do some research? See who's working on these deals, if you recognize any names? You'll have a better understanding than any of us."

"I will try," Ricardo said.

Aidan finished downloading and installing the app and handed the phone back to Ricardo. Ricardo stood up and retrieved his laptop from the messenger bag and sat at the table.

"Since you had your laptop with you, it should be clean, but it's a good idea to run a virus scan anyway," Liam said.

"I'll do the same with ours," Aidan said. "And then I'll do some searching of my own."

They spent the next half hour looking at news articles and editorials for names of Iranian officials involved in the nuclear talks. Ricardo said that he didn't recognize any of them, but Aidan assembled them into a spreadsheet for further research.

As Liam felt the energy from their search dissipating, they were startled by a knock on the suite's door.

"That must be housekeeping," Liam said, and got up to look through the peephole. He turned back to them before he opened the door. "It's not."

Ryan Wood stood there, accompanied by a woman who was almost comically shorter than he was. He invited them into the suite and made the introductions.

"I got a call from a guy in security," Ryan said. "He asked a bunch of questions and I figured out something had happened to you guys.

Ash wanted to come over and make sure Mr. Levy was okay."

"How did you get our room number?" Liam asked.

"Ash is very persuasive," Ryan said.

Ashley was pretty in a petite, librarian way – brown hair in a shoulder-length bob, funky red-framed glasses, a warm smile. She wore a blue and white dress that looked like it had come from the fifties, with a scooped neck and a swirling skirt.

"I got hold of the organizer and convinced her to give the room number to me," she said. "I hope that's all right."

"I am pleased to see you," Ricardo said. "I wish we had a better place to welcome you."

Ryan pulled Liam aside. "What can you tell me about what's going on?"

Liam considered whether he should break client confidentiality. It was a difficult decision, but Ryan Wood might be able to provide additional security if necessary, and his wife was already Ricardo's friend.

Keeping his voice low, Liam explained about the series of threats Ricardo had received, and the way they had triggered a psychotic break. "He's still heavily medicated, and he can be pretty loopy sometimes. At first, we thought he was paranoid, but gradually he's been revealing more information. He had his phone off for a couple of days, and when he turned it on again there were more threats."

"Specific or general?"

"General. Don't speak at the conference. Don't tell people what you know."

Ryan raised his eyebrows. "Can you say what that is?"

Liam gave him a quick rundown of the Argentine bombing, the prosecutor killed in Buenos Aires, the nuclear deal in progress.

Ryan accepted the information in the matter-of-fact way that soldiers took in military briefings, and Liam felt he'd made a good decision in confiding in Ryan.

"He has real information that could kick a hole in that deal?" Ryan asked.

"It depends on whether anyone in a position of power cares, but yeah, he has the smoking gun that points to Iranian involvement in an attack on Argentine citizens on Argentine soil."

Ryan shook his head. "You've got your hands full, don't you? If there's anything I can do to help, let me know. Ash and Ricardo are online friends, and she's very loyal."

"I appreciate it. We should get out of here so the maid can clean up." Liam turned back to the room. "Shall we all go out to dinner?"

Ricardo shook his head. "I cannot go out."

"If the boys are going to hash this out like a military operation we might as well do it over dinner," Ashley said. "Come on, Ricardo."

Liam hid a smile. He hadn't been called a boy in a couple of decades, but from Ashley he didn't mind—it appeared to come out of a fun relationship she had with her husband.

Ricardo shook his head. "I am too nervous to go out."

Ashley threaded an arm through his, and Liam was aware of how different they were—the woman young and short, yet with a commanding personality, while Ricardo was big and bearish and at the same time meek.

"You have lots of guys to protect you," Ashley said to Ricardo. "Plus, I want to talk to you about my research. I want to add some filters to my study to see what kind of effect major events like the AMIA bombing you're going to talk about have on Jewish emigration from across the region, not just the country where they occur."

"It would be interesting to see if there is a cross-national correlation," Ricardo said grudgingly.

Liam turned to Ryan. "We ate lunch at a restaurant on the ground floor of the Coral tower yesterday," he said in a low voice. "Very defensible positions, with tables against the back wall and full view of the entrance and exit."

"I like the way you think," Ryan said. "Let's head there.

As they prepared to walk out, a pair of housekeepers arrived. The first one's eyes opened wide, and Liam was not surprised to see Blake palm her a couple of American bills. If only every problem could be solved so easily.

15 – Strength in Numbers

Aidan covered the rear as they all walked down the hall to the elevator. Ryan and Liam led, with Ashley and Ricardo deep in conversation behind them. Aidan felt like he was in a military operation as they walked from the lobby of their tower to the next, where the restaurant was located. Both Liam and Ryan had assumed defensive posture, their backs straight, their heads swiveling periodically to assess risks. For the moment, at least, Aidan felt secure among them.

They arrived at the restaurant, and the same maître d' was on duty. He guided them to a round table for six near the door to the kitchen, and without saying anything out loud, Liam and Ryan positioned themselves and the other four for maximum security.

Ashley and Ricardo were still deep in conversation about immigration studies and statistics, and Aidan was talking to Blake about a friend of Blake's who had never wanted to settle down. "He's just selfish," Blake said. "He's too caught up in himself to ever commit to someone else. Do you know, he's still bragging that he can wear the same size pants he wore in college?"

The waiter came by, delivered water, but couldn't get anyone's attention. Finally Ryan said, "Ash." He tapped the menu. "Make it happen."

She took over, and Liam was impressed at how smoothly the two of them worked together, when they appeared so different. But then, when people looked at him and Liam, they probably wondered the same thing.

They ate well, platters of fresh fish for Ashley, Blake and Ricardo, steaks for Liam, Aidan and Ryan. "Did you know the Yiddish word for cow is ba-hay-ma?" Aidan said as he cut into his steak. "I'm eating a ba-hay-ma in the Bahamas."

"I wish I spoke more Yiddish," Ashley said. "When I was a kid, my parents only spoke it to each other when they didn't want me to understand."

"My father's family is Sephardic and my mother's is Ashkenazi," Ricardo said. "My mother spoke Yiddish sometimes with her family, but I never understood any of it. And my father's family had been in Argentina so long that no one spoke Ladino."

"This is how languages get lost," Aidan said. "My father's parents spoke to him in Yiddish and he answered in Yiddish, so he could speak and understand. My mother's parents spoke to her in Yiddish and she answered in English, so she could understand a lot more than she could speak. Like Ashley's parents, they only spoke Yiddish to each other when they didn't want me to understand. But I picked up useful curses and useless phrases."

"For example?" Ashley asked.

"If I started a sentence with the word 'if,' my father would say, '*Ef di bubbie volt gehat baytzim, volt zi geven a zeyde*,' which, loosely translated, means 'if your grandmother had balls, she'd be your grandfather'."

Everyone laughed.

"Those old Jews were smart," Ryan said. "They were already thinking about transgender people way back then."

The dinner passed easily, some general conversations, some individual. When they were finished, Blake insisted on signing the charge to his room. "I feel a lot more comfortable knowing that Aidan and Liam have backup," he said. "Not that I don't trust the two of them—we wouldn't be here if I didn't. But there is strength in numbers."

Aidan hoped that he was right. At least Ricardo was much more relaxed after spending time with Ashley.

Ashley and Ryan were going to go for a moonlight walk along the beach, so they said goodbye, and Liam led the way back up to the suite. When they opened the door and saw everything in pristine condition, Aidan felt a wave of exhaustion sweep over him.

Even Blake was yawning. He went over to the round table and began pulling Ricardo's pills out of the small blue bag he had reviewed earlier that evening. "Come over here, sweetheart. Let's get you your pills, and then you can sleep."

Ricardo looked agonized. "I can't think clearly." He crossed his arms over his chest. "I'm not taking those pills anymore. I saw the way Ashley looked at me tonight. Like she can't decide if she should believe me or not, if I'm crazy or telling the truth."

"You can't stop taking your pills," Blake said. "When we get back to Philadelphia, we'll go to the doctor, and see what she says."

"I can't wait that long. I'm done." He got up and stalked to the bedroom.

"What do you think will happen if Ricardo goes off those pills cold turkey?" Aidan asked Blake.

"I have no idea. I'm worried that stopping like that could cause another psychotic break." His shoulders slumped. "I don't know what I could do if that happens. There isn't a hospital in this country that can handle a patient like him. I'd have to get him back home. But how can I do that if he's acting even nuttier than he is now? What if he starts threatening someone, or tries to hurt himself?"

He started to shake, and Aidan went to sit beside him at the table. "We're here to help you, Blake," Aidan said. "We'll figure something out."

"What kind of pills is he taking?" Liam asked.

Blake looked up, and Liam could see that he'd started to cry. Not good. All three of them needed to be on their game if Ricardo was going to act up.

"Quetiapine, haloperidol, and chlorpromazine are anti-psychotics," Blake said, as if he was reading from a medical list. "Fluoxetine is an anti-depressant, brand name Prozac. Eszopiclone for sleep. Atorvastatin for cholesterol, Losartan for high blood pressure. Loratidine, aka Claritin, as a prophylactic because he's prone to sinus headaches. Multivitamin. Folic acid, gingko biloba, Sam-E, omega-3 fatty acids."

He looked at Aidan. "I can't take it if he has another meltdown." Tears welled at the corners of Blake's eyes. "The first time I was so stunned it was like it wasn't real. At least not until I went to see him in the psych ward. It's a lockdown unit, visitors only allowed from 5:30 to 7:00 on Tuesdays and Fridays, and noon to two on Sunday. It was so depressing to go through a metal detector, then have to get buzzed into the unit. I tried to bring him Chinese food one day, and they wouldn't let him have a plastic fork or knife. Just one of those silly spork things."

Aidan caught Liam's eye. Aidan knew that his husband hated this kind of emotional display. Aidan couldn't say that he liked it, but he had spent years teaching students who were unemployed, food or housing insecure, even illegal immigrants, so he had a lot of experience letting someone cry on his shoulder. And he and Blake had years of life experience together. Despite the way Blake had treated him, he couldn't refuse to help.

Blake couldn't hold back the tears anymore. "The first few days he was so confused. He didn't know where he was or why he couldn't come back home. The nurses were either dragon ladies or clueless girls, and there was always this big, hulking security guard on duty. The other patients were crazy as loons. A pregnant girl having a meltdown with her mother because she refused to say who the baby's father was. An old Indian woman in a sari who kept muttering to herself. A skinny tattooed guy who said his name was Jesus."

He stopped to blow his nose. "One day the Jesus guy came up to Ricardo and me and said that he was bisexual, and could he come home with us when Ricardo was discharged."

Aidan held back a laugh at the thought of Blake bringing in a stray. As what? A charity case? A tenant? The third part of a threesome? The Blake he knew, who was still there underneath this man with an unaccustomed display of emotions, would never have agreed to any of those choices.

Aidan put his arm around Blake's shoulders and let him cry. "I was so scared I was going to lose him," Blake said. "That he'd never be well enough to come home, and for the rest of his life I'd be visiting him in awful places like that, only an hour at a time."

"But he got better," Aidan said. "To look at him most of the time, you'd never know anything was wrong with him."

"He's been good with you," Blake said. "Much less paranoid. And he hardly ever takes those damn crystals off to play with them the way he did back in Philadelphia."

"The business he was talking about with the cab driver – about the pope and the Italian singer—has that been part of his psychosis?"

"He fell in love with her when she was a contestant on the Voice Italy," Blake said. "He bought her CD and listened to it as he biked to work. But she didn't fold into his problems until he was ready to leave the hospital."

Blake stood up. "I should go in there with him. I'll try to convince him to take the damn pills. And if he won't, at least I'll be by his side."

Aidan watched him go. Despite all his problems, Ricardo was lucky to have Blake there to care for him. Then Aidan looked over at Liam.

What would he do if something more serious than a broken arm happened to Liam? With every job they took on, there was a chance of serious injury. A bullet to the brain that didn't kill him outright could cause as much mental confusion and anguish as Ricardo was feeling. One to the spine could destroy Liam's physical capabilities, which he had always relied on. His fall from the roof had changed something in Liam, which was why they had pulled back from bodyguard work. What if something more serious happened?

Of course they would stay together. He would stand by Liam no matter what, and he trusted that Liam would do the same.

Liam must have seen something in his face, because he pulled Aidan into a hug. "It's going to be okay. We're here to protect Ricardo and Blake, and now we have Ryan and Ashley to help out."

"Strength in numbers," Aidan said.

Liam nodded. "Strength in numbers."

16 – Paradise

Wednesday morning, Aidan woke to the sound of a muffled argument coming from the living room. He was tempted to roll over and go back to sleep, let Blake and Ricardo work out their troubles on their own, but Liam was awake, too.

"Sounds like trouble in paradise," Liam said.

"Literally," Aidan said. "Not that we've had much chance to enjoy paradise so far."

"We have to get through Ricardo's speech tomorrow," Liam said. "And then we will accompany them to Philadelphia, submit our invoice to the Agence, and go on about our merry way."

Aidan kissed Liam's cheek, pulled on his shorts and walked out to the living room. Ricard was at the table, fumbling with the chains around his neck. "Can you help me with these?" he asked Aidan.

"Sure." Aidan began unhooking and untangling, handing them one by one to Ricardo, who folded them up and placed them in a leather pouch.

"You're not wearing them today?"

"I don't know what I was doing with them," Ricardo said. "Just a bunch of rocks."

Interesting, Aidan thought. Ricardo's eyes were clear and bright, and he seemed more alert than usual. The fact that he was putting away the crystals had to be a good sign, didn't it?

Blake came out of the bedroom and picked up the blue bag of pills. "Are you sure you won't take your pills this morning, love?" he asked.

"I already told you, I don't need them," Ricardo said. "For the first time in ages, my brain is less foggy. I feel more like myself."

"At least take your cholesterol and blood pressure pills," Blake said. "Please?"

"I can take those," Ricardo said. "And my multi-vitamin and the sinus pill. But that's all."

Blake dosed out the pills, and Ricardo took them with a glass of water. "Shall we all go out to breakfast?" he asked. "There's a buffet on the ground floor of the Coral Tower."

"You don't like buffets," Blake said. "You complain that you don't know who has touched your food."

"Don't be ridiculous. We go to Sunday brunch at least once a month at The Shattered Egg back home."

"We haven't been there since you've been sick."

"Well, I'm not feeling sick anymore. And I want to go to breakfast. You can stay here in the room if you want."

To Aidan, Ricardo seemed better without the pills, but who knew how long that would last? Still, he led the way to the restaurant, and accepted the table Liam chose for them. Aidan accompanied him through the buffet line, picking out French toast with a strawberry syrup, hash browns, even a small mushroom and cheese omelet.

As they ate, Ricardo spoke articulately about a session he'd attended the previous day, and there was no mention of singing nuns, crystals or imprisoned fish. Blake looked as taut as a guitar string, as if he was waiting for Ricardo to have a meltdown right there in the hotel restaurant.

Aidan understood his concern. He wished he knew more about mental health. Was this the calm before the storm, a brief period of sanity before even more craziness popped up?

After breakfast, Blake returned to the suite, Liam resumed his post outside the conference center, and Aidan and Ricardo took their usual seats along the side of the room.

As the first session began, Aidan watched Ricardo closely, trying to see if the effect of stopping his pills had been short-lived. Ricardo listened intently to the speaker, and for the first time since the conference kicked off, began writing comments and questions in a pocket notebook.

After a few minutes of watching Ricardo, Aidan pulled out his phone and Googled "stopping anti-psychotic medications."

The general advice was to taper off slowly, because stopping too quickly could cause a relapse of symptoms. However, he did find some reports by individuals who stated that their symptoms, such as paranoia and delusions, went away as soon as they stopped taking their medications.

Which group would Ricardo fall into? It was impossible to tell. Aidan wasn't a psychiatrist, and though they'd spent four days together by then, he hardly knew Ricardo and had no basis of prior behavior to judge against.

Blake did, though. Aidan made a mental note to talk to Blake and see how he thought Ricardo was doing.

At the mid-morning break, Ricardo got up and walked over to Ashley. He kissed her cheek and she squeezed his hand, and they began a fast-paced conversation in Spanish, which several other participants joined.

The dark circles under Ricardo's eyes were still there but he smiled frequently. The El Greco Jesus effect had faded, and he looked more handsome, more energized. He'd put on a dark blue polo shirt and khaki slacks and appeared a step closer to a guy enjoying a tropical location. Aidan could see more clearly than ever why Blake had been attracted to Ricardo – his loose dark curls matched his easy smile, and his body language was open and friendly.

He returned to sit beside Aidan during the second speaker, but it was obvious that the topic didn't interest him. He opened his messenger bag and pulled out a sheaf of papers that appeared to be the text of his speech the next day.

Aidan was fascinated as Ricardo's pen danced across the page, editing. Aidan noticed the way he crossed out words that expressed uncertainty, liked "it seems to me," and made his argument stronger, more focused. He couldn't follow everything on the page, because Ricardo worked too fast, but by Ricardo's actions Aidan could tell his client's brain appeared much more focused.

After that session, he and Ashley joined a couple of other attendees for lunch. Aidan and Liam sat nearby.

"How's he seem this morning?" Liam asked.

Aidan described the effects he'd noticed, from Ricardo's better physical well-being to his revisions to his notes.

"He's not writing gibberish?" Liam asked.

Aidan shook his head. "I don't think so. I looked over his shoulder, and he appears to be making his points stronger."

"Good. Hope the effect lasts." Liam finished his sandwich and pushed his plate away. "Yesterday, whoever is after Ricardo tossed our suite. We have to assume that he didn't find what he was looking for, because Ricardo kept the proof he has of the Iranian government involvement in his messenger bag."

Aidan nodded. "What's his next step? If I were in his shoes, I'd recognize that the proof is in the bag, and I'd go after Ricardo and steal the bag."

"That's what I'd do, too," Liam said. "We need to be especially vigilant wherever Ricardo goes. If this guy is smart, and there's nothing to say he isn't, he's established that you and I are on the job. So that means he has to separate Ricardo from us."

"He could have an associate here at the conference," Aidan said, thinking out loud. "Someone Ricardo expects to trust, who might pull him aside for a private conference. And then the bad guy swoops in."

"Don't leave his side," Liam said. "Even if he has to use the bathroom."

They'd had clients in this situation before, and the fact that they had been able to be proactive in those past jobs and keep the client out of danger made Aidan feel more secure.

They boxed Ricardo and his colleagues in as they left the restaurant, Liam in front, Aidan behind. They tried to be as inconspicuous as possible, but Aidan noticed that Ashley

Goldstein-Wood looked from Liam to Aidan and back.

Ricardo was engaged in the first afternoon speaker's presentation, not touching his notes. Aidan used the time to speculate on when Ricardo might be most vulnerable, outside of bathroom breaks. So far, they'd been successful at keeping him reined in; his paranoia made Ricardo unwilling to leave their side. But now that he felt better, would he be less willing to listen to them?

At the break between the afternoon sessions, Ashley Goldstein-Wood came up to Aidan, who had gotten up to get water. Ricardo stayed in his seat, swiveled around to speak with an attendee who had been sitting behind them the whole conference.

"Ricardo looks so much better today than he did yesterday," Ashley said. "He's like a different person."

"I think he's being energized by the sessions," Aidan said, unwilling to spill the beans of Ricardo's mental illness to Ashley. "It helped that he got to talk to you yesterday after the break-in at our suite. You calmed him down."

"If I had any part, it was a small one," she said. "Any word on who was responsible?"

Aidan looked back at Ricardo, who was still engaged with the man behind him, and shook his head. "A few of the things Liam and I brought with us were stolen, but nothing of Ricardo's or Blake's. The police are treating it like a random burglary—like it's our fault that Blake booked us into a fancy suite."

"Ryan told me about a conversation he had with Liam." The dress she wore was similar to the one from the day before, with a low-cut neck, short sleeves and a swirly skirt, but it was in a shimmering green, and she wore flat sandals in the same color. "And last night at dinner, he was acting very strangely. Talking about lost gods and singing nuns. But today he's different, so much better."

"I don't want to get too detailed and violate Ricardo's privacy, but I agree with you, he's a lot better today than he has been."

She thought for a moment. "In the conference notes, I read that Ricardo says he has proof that Iran was involved in the AMIA bombing. You think that's why he's been threatened?"

"He has. The threats upset him, and he had a kind of breakdown this fall."

Ashley nodded. "Ryan told me. The poor thing."

"He's on a lot of medication, so it has been hard to tell sometimes if he's imagining things or if the threats are real. But he has gotten some new threats, and we think that whoever broke into the suite was looking for the proof he has to back up his speech tomorrow."

"He's still going to give his presentation? Despite these threats?"

"He's determined."

She nodded, with a determined smile on her face. "Props to him. Sometimes I get irritated that my work flies under the radar so much, but now I'm grateful."

They returned to their separate seats. By then, Ricardo had finished his conversation with the man behind him and was once again reviewing his notes for his speech the next day. He seemed happier with it, because he wasn't making big changes anymore.

During the final session, Ricardo alternated between listening to the speaker and making the occasional note. When the session ended, Ricardo turned to Aidan. "I'd like to go to the event this evening. Will you or Liam be able to go with me?"

"I'll have to check with Liam, but I don't think it will be a problem. Remind me what the event is?"

"It's an open forum for researchers to share their results and get feedback. There are a lot of junior faculty here who don't have the credentials yet to be on a panel or give a presentation. This is a chance for them to get up and speak."

Ricardo texted Blake, who agreed to meet them in the lobby for dinner, and Aidan, Liam and Ricardo walked out of the convention center together.

"You can do this evening, can't you?" Liam asked, when Aidan brought up the event that Ricardo wanted to attend. "I'm antsy from standing around all day. I want to get in a swim, if you think you won't need me outside."

"This is a smaller session, and whoever's after Ricardo has no way of knowing he'll be there. As long as we're alert on our way in, I think we'll be fine."

"I want to try the Bahamian restaurant near the marina," Ricardo said, as Blake joined them. "We're here, so we should sample the native cuisine."

Aidan knew that Blake liked his food fancy, preferring an elegant French restaurant to a street front taco stand, for example, but he agreed without complaint. As they walked, Aidan pulled Blake aside. "How do you think Ricardo is doing today?"

Blake blew out a long breath. "I'm scared he'll have a relapse, but right now, it's like having the old Ricardo back. He's so much more outgoing and articulate, the way he used to be, now that he's off those meds. How do you think he is?"

"I don't have the frame of reference you do, but he does seem about a thousand percent better than he was yesterday."

The Bahamian restaurant was in a quaint building designed to look like one of the old-time houses on the island, painted a shining yellow. White gingerbread trim hung under the eaves, and roll-down shutters kept out the heat and light.

Ricardo wanted to sit outside, so Liam negotiated with the hostess for a four-top along the back wall, protected from the street by another row of tables and a low hedge. They sat on brightly colored wooden chairs beneath a ceiling fan with blades the shape of palm leaves.

For the first time on that trip, Aidan started to enjoy himself, lulled by the breeze from the marina and the gentle reggae music floating through the speakers. In front of them, families and couples strolled or posed for selfies. Just what a vacation should be.

The four of them shared an appetizer of conch fritters and Aidan was surprised to see Blake dig in, dipping them into a spicy tomato sauce. The old Blake would never have deigned to eat such simple food or use his fingers to eat.

But he hadn't known the old Blake for ten years, he reminded himself. People changed. And look at what a metamorphosis Ricardo had undergone in only one day without his anti-psychotics and anti-depressants.

They talked about restaurants and museums in Philadelphia, the beaches of Corsica and the Hagia Sophia mosque in Istanbul. Then Ricardo asked, "You went to Chechnya last year? You were not frightened to go to such a homophobic place?"

"That's why we went," Liam said. "The son of our friend, also gay, was traveling there, trying to help gay men who wanted to flee, and he disappeared for a few days. We flew out to look for him."

"I read about a fire at a prison there, where they were suspected to house gay men," Ricardo said. "Was that your doing?"

"We didn't burn the prison," Liam said. "The government did that. I'll say it was empty by the time they did."

Ricardo pressed for more details, but Liam declined to get specific. "What we do for clients remains confidential, even after the job is done."

Blake nodded at that, and Aidan recognized the lawyer in him rising to the top.

By the time they finished, they had to hurry back to the convention center so Ricardo could attend the evening session. They followed signs to a room off the main corridor, where chairs had been set up in a semi-circle around a central podium.

Blake and Liam left them, Blake to work up in the suite and Liam to head for a swim. Aidan was surprised at how interesting he found the speakers. Their presentations were restricted to ten minutes, and another ten for question and answers, and that was enough information to pique Aidan's brain. One young man wearing a yarmulke over incongruously bright red hair was researching the effect of Chabad, the

Orthodox proselytizers, in Miami Beach, Rio de Janeiro, and Buenos Aires. Another was compiling a textbook about the contributions of Jewish pioneers to democracy in Latin America. And another was writing a biography of Tania the Guerrilla, an Argentine-born communist revolutionary and spy who had been born Jewish, and was active in various Latin American revolutionary movements.

Ricardo was an eager participant, asking questions and applauding speakers, and Aidan relaxed. Ricardo's presentation would be the next day, and once he'd spoken his piece and provided his proof, there should be no reason to threaten him.

Maybe they'd be able to continue to enjoy a bit of paradise before they left.

17 – Strange Intimacy

Wednesday evening, while Blake worked in the suite and Aidan and Ricardo attended the presentation, Liam performed a dozen sun salutations beside the pool, then swam twenty laps, until he had worked out all the tension in his body that came from standing on alert all day. When he returned to the suite, he took a quick shower and joined Blake in the living room.

Blake opened a bottle of white wine and poured glasses for himself and Liam. Knowing he was still on duty, even though Aidan was watching Ricardo, Liam sipped his wine, though he noticed that Blake chugged his quickly and poured a second glass.

Blake leaned forward, his glass gripped in his right hand. "You're a lucky man."

Liam smiled, his lips tightly shut. This kind of small talk with the client was one of his least favorite parts of any assignment, and whenever possible he deferred to Aidan. But Aidan wasn't there. "How so?" he asked.

"I didn't realize what I had with Aidan until he was gone. You know, of course, that I embarrassed myself by chasing after him to Tunisia."

Liam remembered Blake appearing at the door of the house behind the Bar Mamounia, looking tired and bedraggled. Yet despite his appearance then he was bossy, offering only the simplest apology for kicking Aidan out, and telling Aidan it was time to come back.

Liam's heart had been in his stomach as he waited for Aidan's response. Would this man he'd begun to fall in love with give up on him and return to the luxurious life he'd enjoyed in Philadelphia?

Fortunately for Liam, Aidan had chosen him, and Liam had been grateful ever since. "You did what you thought was right," Liam said.

"I spent the whole plane ride back to Philadelphia mentally kicking myself." Blake shook his head. "I went back over all the things Aidan had done for me, and how stupid and selfish I'd been."

"You've managed since then."

Blake smiled grimly. "It was a tough road. Aidan spoiled me. I didn't know where he took my dry cleaning, where he bought the chocolate croissants I liked. I felt like a kid, learning to take care of myself all over again."

Liam thought that had been good for Blake, but he didn't say anything.

Blake sat back against the sofa. "I spent half my time angry with myself for kicking him out, and the other half of the time angry with Aidan for not coming back with me."

Liam couldn't resist hearing about his husband's relationship with Blake from the other side. "How did you and Aidan meet?" he asked.

Blake looked embarrassed. "You've probably already heard the story. I had an older friend, my gay mentor if you will. He thought I was wound too tight and needed to relax and get laid, so he dragged me to this gay bar in Center City. I was horrified when I walked in—most of the men were in their fifties and sixties, desperately trying to look younger with artful haircuts and tight-fitting shirts. And everyone was singing along with the piano player to show tunes."

He shuddered. "It was everything I thought was awful about being gay. These old men, alone, following every stereotype. They made catty comments and called gay men 'she' and 'her' and I was waiting until I could slip out." He smiled. "Then Aidan came in with a friend, and even though they were the youngest guys in the room, they jumped right in, singing along with 'I Heard it Through the Grapevine.' I caught Aidan's eye and he winked at me, and I had to get to know him."

"Aidan remembers that same song," Liam said.

"For years, we used to laugh and call it our song," Blake said. "I hated sentimentality and thought I was being ironic. But then after a while I realized the song did mean something to both of us."

The evening's fireworks began outside. With the door slightly open, Liam could hear the whistles and booms. He was glad he wasn't outside with the client, worrying about what someone with bad intentions could do under the cover of that noise and spectacle.

"I walked over and gave him my card when the song ended," Blake continued. "He looked at it like I'd handed him a dog turd, and I knew I had to change my game if I wanted to win him. After the next song, I asked him if he wanted to get some dinner. I said that I knew the maître d' at Le Bec Fin, the best French restaurant in the city, and I could get us a table easily."

Blake laughed. "He said he couldn't let a guy take him to a restaurant that fancy for a first date—how could we ever follow that up? Instead we went to a place called The Commissary, where my office ordered sandwiches for lunch, and we ate and we talked, and then he said he had an early class the next morning, so he had to call it a night."

He shook his head. "I couldn't get him out of my head. He was adorable back then—skinny as a rail, cute as a button, all those clichés. He had spent a year teaching English in Thailand, and he was picking up some classes and private clients to make money to travel again. He was so passionate about everything—the places he'd been or wanted to go, his students, the world and politics and injustice."

"He's still that guy," Liam said.

"I took advantage of his good nature. I see that now. He was so eager to please me, and in my defense, eager to learn anything he could. I sent him to cooking classes and flower arranging and massage lessons and God knows what else. I wouldn't let him teach night classes after a while, so when I got home he'd be there with dinner on the table. He had the opportunity to interview for a full-time job teaching ESL at the community college in Philadelphia, and I discouraged him from applying because I wanted to be the whole focus of his life."

He sighed. "Gradually, things changed. I started calling him my ball and chain, and resenting him for being clingy, when I was the one who fostered that attitude in the first place. When I was out of town on business a couple of times, I cheated on him. The sex was so – different – and I convinced myself that I was silly to stay tied to one man."

"That's when you kicked him out," Liam said.

"I want to say it was the stupidest thing I ever did, and it certainly ranks up there, but if I hadn't, he wouldn't have met you, and I wouldn't have met Ricardo, and where would we all be then?"

"That's the way he looks at it, too," Liam said. "Though it took him a while to realize that I'm a different guy from you, and that I expected him to be himself, not my personal assistant."

Liam leaned forward. He felt the wine acting on his system, but he couldn't resist asking, "How do you manage to be different with Ricardo?"

"I promised myself that if I had a chance with someone else, I'd try to do better. It's a work in progress, I'll tell you. After I got back to Philadelphia, I had a couple of dates but my bitterness kept popping up and no one was willing to see me a second time. Then I met Ricardo at an event on doing business with Latin America, where one of my clients was speaking. We started to talk during the cocktail hour, and then we sat next to each other, whispering comments back and forth."

He smiled. "After the event was over, he asked if I wanted to go to dinner with him so we could continue our conversation. I agreed, even though I was supposed to go out with my client and some of his colleagues. I didn't even know Ricardo was gay then, just that he was fascinating and that we were clicking on all cylinders."

It was weirdly intriguing to listen to Blake's romance with Aidan and Ricardo, like eating a forbidden fruit. "Can I ask you a very personal question?" Liam asked.

Blake picked up his glass of wine and emptied it. "Why not?"

"Are you circumcised?"

Blake nearly choked on the last of his wine. "Whatever makes you ask that?"

"I'm not, and Aidan has this minor obsession with my foreskin. And I figured you, with two Jewish guys in a row, you might, you know…" He stumbled. He didn't know what he was asking, but it was something that he'd been wondering about.

"In the spirit of full disclosure, I am six inches, cut," he said. "As they say in the personal ads, or at least as they did when I was single." He poured himself another glass of wine and held the bottle up to Liam.

He shook his head. He'd already opened up more than he intended. "You're paying me to have a clear head and look after you and your husband."

"I appreciate that." Blake took a sip of wine. "Neither of my parents were religious, though supposedly my father is descended from Huguenots, French Protestants. When I met Aidan, I was fascinated by his commitment to Judaism—it seemed exotic to me. Ricardo feels the same way, and his work is even more entwined with his religion. I guess it was the passion they both felt that impressed me."

Blake leaned forward. "Do you dock?"

Liam felt a flush rising on his cheeks. What he and Aidan did in the bedroom was none of Blake's business, but he had to admit he'd opened the door himself. "Sometimes," he admitted. "It's strange to fetishize a little circle of skin, but Aidan likes it, and it doesn't matter to me."

Liam regretted that he hadn't gotten fully dressed after his shower. He was shirtless, wearing only the pair of gym shorts Aidan had bought at the Penn bookstore, and he felt his dick unfurling. He shifted position so that it wouldn't be obvious to Blake.

"Aidan was my first serious boyfriend," Blake said. "Was he

yours?"

Liam nodded. "I was in the military under Don't Ask, Don't Tell."

"I don't have that excuse. I was in a closet of my own making. I grew up watching those catty gay men on TV like Paul Lynde and being horrified by them. I didn't realize there were ordinary guys who liked guys until long after I graduated from law school. And by then, I was embarrassed at being a late bloomer. I didn't lose my virginity until I was twenty-six."

Liam was relieved that Aidan and Ricardo came in then, which put an end to the strange intimacy that had developed between him and Blake. "Oh good, you saved me some wine," Aidan said, as he sat beside Liam. He leaned over and kissed his husband's cheek, then reached for the bottle.

"I will have a glass, too," Ricardo said. "Now that I am not taking those lousy pills."

They finished the bottle. Blake was already quite tipsy and wanted to open another, but Liam refused. "We should all get to bed," he said. "Ricardo has a big day tomorrow."

"Yes, my speech," Ricardo said, raising his nearly empty glass in a toast. The four of them clinked glasses. "To my success, and to satisfaction for the families of the dead."

Liam felt guilty that he'd been relaxed on duty, drinking wine and sharing true confessions with Blake, and he was glad to hustle Aidan back to their room and shut the door.

"How long were you and Blake drinking?" Aidan asked.

"Long enough. Too long, I suppose."

Aidan looked up at him, smiling. "Were you talking about me?"

Liam nodded. "And Ricardo. How Blake is trying to be different with Ricardo than he was with you."

"There's something more," Aidan said, staring at him. "Something you're not telling me. Don't tell me you and Blake…" His eyes widened.

"Are you out of your mind? Though we did, um, share some information."

Aidan walked right up to him. "What kind of information? You weren't talking to my ex about having sex with me, were you?"

Liam felt himself blushing. "Not exactly. But I'll admit tongues were loosened."

"Oh, Liam. You've been a bad boy." He reached behind his husband and slapped Liam's meaty ass with the palm of his hand. Liam flinched, but didn't make a move to stop him.

"What did you tell him?"

"I was curious that the two important men in his life were Jewish, and I asked if he was circumcised."

"You didn't!" Aidan slapped Liam's ass again. "He is. And just so you know, your dick is thicker than his."

"He said he was six inches, cut."

"Oh. My. God. You are so going to have to make this up to me." Aidan kicked off his deck shoes, unbuttoned his slacks, and dropped them and his boxers to the floor. "On your knees, sailor."

Aidan's dick was already stiff—and so was Liam's, he had to admit. As it had been for part of his conversation with Blake.

He did as commanded, getting down on his knees on the carpeted floor. He licked Aidan's dick up and down, then took it in his mouth. "Yeah, that's right," Aidan said. "Show me you're a better cocksucker than Blake Chennault."

Bringing Aidan's ex into the room was a weird aphrodisiac for both of them. Liam licked and sucked Aidan's dick, bringing him almost to the edge, then he pulled off and stood up.

"What?" Aidan demanded.

"He asked if we docked," Liam said with a sly smile. He dropped his gym shorts and pulled Aidan's dick close to his own. Then he tugged the foreskin up and Aidan guided his dick into the opening.

"I get the feeling Blake wasn't the most open lover in the world," Liam said. "Pretty vanilla?"

"The very definition of a vanilla lover," Aidan said, tugging Liam's foreskin over the head of his dick, feeling so connected to him. "He thought ass fucking was unclean, and the most he'd ever do was tease a finger around my hole. Once he read somewhere about water sports and decided he wanted to try pissing on me. He got me naked in the tub, and he stood over me—but he couldn't make himself do it."

Liam leaned down and kissed Aidan. They didn't need Blake looking over their shoulders or hanging around in their brains. All they needed was each other. He wrapped his fist around the place where their dicks met, under his foreskin, and began rubbing back and forth. The closure of his foreskin around Aidan's dick created a kind of suction that amplified his motion, and quickly he felt his orgasm rising.

Aidan wrapped his hand around Liam's and together they rubbed and squeezed until Liam couldn't hold back anymore, and he began to shoot. He held firm to Aidan's dick, continuing to rub it automatically, until Aidan shot, too. The force of his ejaculation pushed Liam's dick back, and they were both spurting into the air and onto each other.

Liam's body sagged, and Aidan wrapped his arms around Liam and held him close. Liam leaned down and kissed Aidan's hair, and Aidan licked his collarbone.

Then Aidan slapped Liam's ass one more time.

18 – Life in Fear

When Aidan woke Thursday morning, he went into the bathroom, then pulled on a pair of gym shorts and walked out into the living room of the suite. Ricardo was pacing around muttering to himself, and Aidan was immediately worried he'd regressed.

But instead he looked at Aidan and said, "Do you and Liam share clothes?"

"Good morning to you, too," Aidan said.

"It's just, I recognize those shorts. They're the ones Liam was wearing last night. I noticed the Penn crest on them. I guess you must have several pair."

Aidan was embarrassed, though he didn't know why. Perhaps there was something intimate about sharing clothes—especially ones that had already been worn.

By his husband. As they began to have sex.

"What do you want to do about breakfast this morning?" Aidan asked, changing the subject.

"Perhaps I will have a roll from the continental breakfast. I am a bit nervous."

"Missing your pills?"

"No, not at all. I've been rehearsing my speech. I hope it will go well."

"I'm sure it will."

Blake came out of the bedroom then. "I'd like to hear your speech today, sweetheart."

"If you would like. They have a special one-session guest pass you can register for at the door."

They agreed that Blake would work in the suite until the time of Ricardo's presentation, and he would join them at eleven. He went back into the bedroom, and Liam, Aidan and Ricardo left for the conference center.

Ricardo was stressed as they waited for the elevator, and then rode down to the lobby, but he manifested it differently than when he'd been medicated. Then, he'd been rabbity, ready to bolt, scanning the area around him like a soldier on point. Thursday morning, however, his stress was internal; he took a lot of deep breaths and seemed to be lost in thought most of the time.

Aidan was glad when they got into the convention center and settled in their usual seats. Ricardo ignored the first speaker, an Israeli with a guttural accent. Instead he pulled out his lecture notes, mouthing words and phrases inaudibly.

The Israeli was almost finished when Aidan noticed Shadrach, the security chief, enter and begin to walk down the side corridor.

That can't be good, he thought.

Then he saw Liam behind the man, and he knew something was wrong. "We have to go," Aidan whispered to Ricardo. "Close your laptop and let's get moving."

"But I am the next speaker," Ricardo protested.

By then Shadrach had reached the podium, and politely moved the speaker away. Liam reached them and put his hand on Ricardo's shoulder. "Up, now," he said.

Aidan grabbed Ricardo's laptop, closed it, and rose with Ricardo.

"We have received a threat against this facility," Shadrach said, in his easy-going island accent. "I have to ask you all to evacuate the premises immediately. There are security guards at the exit to help you."

Ricardo followed Liam, with Aidan behind him, up the side staircase as the audience erupted in chatter and panic. Men and women stood, pushing their way out of the center of the room. A woman began to cry, while others walked and texted at the same time, occasionally bumping into each other.

"Please, please, be calm," Shadrach pleaded from the podium, but his words fell on deaf ears.

Aidan realized that many of the people in the room were Jews, so they had generations of fear built into their DNA, from slavery by the Egyptians, raids by Cossacks, roundups by the Nazis. The cacophony in the room was deafening, the desperation palpable.

Aidan was glad Liam was so large he could bulldoze a way through to the exit, and they spilled out into the hallway.

"What is going on?" Ricardo asked, tugging on Liam's sleeve.

"Let's get out of here first." Liam led them down a hallway to the lobby of the second tower. There was no sense of urgency among the people around them; clearly the bomb threat had not been broadcast to the hotel at large.

They passed a police officer with a German shepherd on a leash.

Aidan saw the dog and said, "Bomb dog?"

"Probably. I saw Shadrach on his way in and he told me a bomb threat had come in via email."

"Why isn't the whole hotel being evacuated then?" Ricardo asked.

"Shadrach told me the convention center can be isolated by fireproof doors," Liam said. "Even so, I'd rather not be near there."

"Should I call Blake?" Aidan asked.

"Text him and tell him there's a delay, and we'll let him know when he should come down," Liam said.

Aidan sent the text and noted that it had been received and read. He put his phone in his pocket and focused on the gentle Bahamian music spilling out of the loudspeakers, and the fact that no one else around them felt any sense of urgency. "Do you think there is a bomb?" he asked.

"I doubt it. If you want to blow a place up, why notify people in advance? Bomb threats are usually duds. From what I know, only five to ten percent result in the discovery of real bombs. And in those cases, it's an accomplice who gets cold feet and calls in the threat. This is probably an attempt to disrupt the conference, but you can never be one hundred percent sure. I'd rather err on the side of caution."

A group of Chinese tourists followed a leader holding up a paddle with the Bahamian flag on it. Liam darted around them, and then a family with five small children, each holding a pool float in the shape of a different animal.

Liam led them outside, past the valets and the line of taxi cabs, to a coral-stone walkway lined with leafy trees. It was cool and shady there, and Aidan felt safe.

"Do you think this threat was aimed at me?" Ricardo asked.

"My gut reaction is yes," Liam said. "Whoever it is wants to frighten you away from speaking."

"It is not what happens, but how you respond that matters. I will not be silenced." He looked more determined than frightened, and Aidan saw a strength in him that had been hidden by all those pills and the craziness.

"Let's see what happens with this threat first," Liam said. They moved slowly down the walkway. In the distance, Aidan heard the sound of children playing.

They walked slowly, in and out of dappled shade, for nearly half an hour, until Liam's phone buzzed with an incoming text. He looked at it, then said, "That was from Ryan Wood. The hotel has announced that the premises are clear and the convention is going to continue."

"Then we need to return." Ricardo turned back, and Aidan pivoted to keep up with him.

"After your speech, we should report the threats you received to the Bahamian police," Liam said, as they walked back toward the hotel, Ricardo leading.

"The police?" Ricardo stopped and looked at Liam. "What can they do?"

"For starters, they can see if these messages you've gotten have any of the same attributes of the bomb threat. Did it come in by phone? Email? Maybe from one of the addresses used here. Maybe the language will match."

"I don't want to go to the police," Ricardo said. "You can't trust them in a country like this. They could be in league with the Iranians.

As soon as they have me in custody, they'll turn me over. Or worse."

"We'll talk about it later."

They began walking again, out of the shaded walkway, through the congestion of the driveway where a tour bus spewed out a seemingly endless line of overweight Americans with tropical shirts and nascent sunburns.

Liam led them back into the lobby. Halfway down the hallway to the convention center, he waved at Ryan Wood and his wife. "I want to see what Ryan has been able to find out," he said, and began striding toward the couple. Aidan and Ricardo followed like obedient ducklings.

"Hey, Ryan." Liam nodded to Ashley. "You hear anything more about the bomb threat?"

"I spotted one of the security guys who looked ex-military and went up to talk to him," Ryan said. "He said he couldn't say much, but he did know there had been an emailed threat to the convention center address."

Aidan admired his initiative; that's what Liam would have done. In the course of living with Liam, and seeing him around other former military men, Aidan had learned that there was a way that men carried themselves if they had served in the armed forces, something you could recognize if you knew what you were looking for. They were always aware of their surroundings. They walked with a purpose, stood at ease in a power stance. In many cases they kept their hair military short, wore sunglasses, and were excessively polite in conversation, using sir and ma'am regularly.

The five of them walked back to the convention center together.

Hotel security and Bahamian police stood at the doors, only allowing those with pre-registered conference badges to enter. Shadrach had disappeared, and even when Aidan protested to one of the police officers that he had purchased a guest pass, he was told that for security purposes, guest passes had been invalidated for the rest of the day.

Aidan was irritated, but he understood the initiative. If their bad guy was getting desperate enough, he might have bought a last-minute pass and positioned himself inside the auditorium. Shadrach and his team were smart enough to anticipate that.

"Blake will not be able to hear me either," Ricardo said. "But that is the way of things." He smiled at Aidan and Liam. "I will be fine."

"I hate to let you go on your own," Liam said. "What if something else happens?"

"I cannot live my life in fear," Ricardo said, and Aidan admired his courage. "I will see you after my speech."

19 – Waiting Game

Liam watched Ricardo show his badge to one of the white-uniformed security guards and enter the lobby of the conference center. He was either very brave or oblivious to the threat—or a combination of both.

"Why don't you go upstairs and fill Blake in on what's going on," Liam said to Aidan. "I'll hang around here." He nodded toward Ryan Wood. "I don't think Ryan's going anywhere either."

"Be careful, sweetheart." Aidan leaned up and kissed Liam's cheek, and Liam felt the moisture from the kiss against his dry skin. He and Aidan didn't generally practice much public display of affection, unless they were in a safe place, because why give random assholes a chance to make a scene? But at a time of high tension like this, Liam was glad of the physical contact. In the military he had learned how fragile life was, how quickly a friend or a fellow soldier could disappear from his life. He was determined that if anything ever happened to him or Aidan, their last contact would be a positive one.

He squeezed Aidan's hand in his. "I will be. You too."

Aidan left, and the last of the attendees trickled into the lobby of the conference center. Then the guard closed the door, stationing himself outside.

Ryan stood at the other end of the shallow lobby that separated the conference center from the hotel corridor, which ebbed and flowed with families and hotel staff.

Liam walked over to Ryan. "How's Ashley holding up?"

"She lives in a different world from you and me," Ryan said. "Academia. I'm not saying there aren't threats—her college gets at least one bomb threat every semester, usually around final exam weeks. And last year the ex-boyfriend of a student came on campus, tracked the girl down, and shot her and two of her classmates."

"That's pretty scary."

"It should be. But Ash lives in her head, you know. More concerned with the fate of Jews in Latin America than about her own personal safety. It drives me nuts, but I can only do what I can do."

It was a lot like Liam's world view, though he was glad that Aidan was more aware of threats in the real world than Ashley appeared to be.

A pair of young Bahamian women with name tags herded a group of kids from about six to ten along the corridor. Kids were speaking over each other, about the aquarium and fish they were going to see. "I want to see lots of big sharks!" one boy crowed, in a flat, Midwestern accent.

"They'll eat you up," another boy said.

"Not if I push you in the water first," the shark boy responded. They started tussling, and one of the girls had to stop and separate them. It took a couple of minutes before the group had moved beyond them.

Ryan looked at Liam. "How do you manage, you and Aidan? Aren't you worried about him every time something happens on a job?"

"I am. My biggest fear is that if it comes down to saving a client or

Aidan, I'll save Aidan, and that violates my duty to the client."

"Wouldn't want to trade places with you," Ryan said. "I made my vows to Ash at our wedding. I knew about her family history, the way they were chased from country to country, and I promised to protect her against all enemies, foreign and domestic."

"The Oath of Allegiance," Liam said. "Really? In your wedding vows?"

"Ash had to swear to it when she became a legal permanent resident of the United States," Ryan said. "I swiped the language from there because I wanted to reinforce it. That after being in the military and vowing to protect the United States, I was making that same oath to her."

He looked at Liam. "You guys are married, right? Did you write your own vows?"

"We did. But we focused on the love stuff." Liam felt himself blushing, but there was no harm in repeating to Ryan what he had said to Aidan in front of a crowd of their friends and relatives. "I was pretty conflicted about being gay for a long time, and then I was in the military during Don't Ask, Don't Tell. I told Aidan that he had showed me that I deserved love, and that he'd given me more than I could ever have hoped for."

"That's sweet. Ash went all sentimental on me, going back to the first day we met when we were in college. She all but accused me of dipping her pigtails in an inkwell."

Liam laughed. "As if there are inkwells these days, or girls who wear their hair in pigtails."

Ryan laughed with him. "Yeah, but the gist of it was true. I fell hard for her right away and I didn't know how to express myself. I guess we're just a pair of big lugs, huh?"

"That is true."

They stood quietly for a while, watching the traffic come and go, both of them wary of any noise that might erupt from the conference room. At least the door and walls were solid, and between the two of them and the security guard at the door, there was little chance of anyone getting in from the outside.

"You said you spoke to one of the guards about the bomb threat. Any way you think we can get a copy of that email?"

"Why do you want to see that?" Ryan asked.

"There's a distinctive pattern to the grammar errors in the messages Ricardo has received." He explained what Aidan had said about the lack of articles.

Ryan eyed him. "I wouldn't have taken you for a grammar nerd."

"That's all down to Aidan. He's got a master's in teaching English as a second language, and he was a teacher before we met. He also pointed out spelling errors in the domain name that the messages come from. Something about using an email anonymizer?"

"Yeah, I know a little about that. I work in procurement now for a military contractor and we get periodic training sessions on email security."

"That what you did in the Navy – procurement?"

"Among other things. Ash and I met in college, and she got her master's and PhD while I was in the Navy. When I got out, we both agreed it was going to be hardest for her to get a tenure-track teaching job, so I'd follow wherever she went and look for a job when we got there."

They talked idly for a while, and Liam checked his watch. It had been nearly forty-five minutes by then, about the length that had been allocated to Ricardo for his presentation.

A few minutes later, he and Ryan heard the crowd inside the auditorium erupt in applause. There was obviously a question and answer period after the speech, as a few people trickled out. Every time the door opened Liam heard Ricardo's amplified voice, sometimes in English and sometimes in Spanish.

Finally, there was another round of applause, and the attendees began to stream out, talking animatedly to each other in a mix of languages. Ryan and Liam tried to get into the room, but the hotel security stopped them once again.

Liam looked around the guard and saw Ricardo still at the podium, speaking to a group of others, including Ashley. It took another ten minutes before Ricardo and Ashley came out, the last of the room to leave.

"How did it go?" Ryan asked.

"Ricardo was awesome!" Ashley said. "His speech was so well-organized and supported with screens of data. Dozens of people came up afterwards to tell him how great he was."

"And now the information is in the public hands," Ricardo said. "My work is finished." He smiled. "At least on that project."

"Hopefully, that means that no one will have any reason to

threaten you," Liam said.

They called Blake and Aidan to join them for a celebratory lunch at a sandwich and salad restaurant in one of the farther towers. Liam, Ryan and Ashley got there first, and Liam scanned the crowds for his husband's familiar face, his build and the way he walked. He spotted Aidan, with Blake by his side, the two of them talking animatedly, like old friends.

Which of course they were. They had shared nearly eleven years together, and despite the circumstances of their breakup, they had to have so much shared experience.

He and Aidan were approaching the point when his time with Aidan will outpace that of Aidan's and Blake's. Another year or so. And yet, he couldn't imagine a time when they would separate; his heart told him that he would spend the rest of his life with Aidan.

Liam felt an obligation to remain watchful, though, so he made sure they sat at a secure table with a view to the exits. Blake slid into a seat next to Ricardo. "I am sorry I had to miss your speech. I want to hear it later, or at least read it."

Ricardo smiled and squeezed Blake's hand. "I am very happy with what I did," Ricardo said. "And I appreciate how much you did for me when I was sick. I would not be here if not for you."

Liam caught Aidan's eye, and they both smiled.

While they waited for their food, Liam checked his email and found that Louis Fleck had managed to get hold of the text of the email threat to the conference and had attached it. "Take a look at this," he said, handing the phone to Aidan. "Doesn't this look a lot like the threats that Ricardo received?"

Aidan took the phone and stared at the screen. Then he pointed. "The writer is using the correct article this time—but now he's switching between the past and the present tense."

"Why does that matter?" Ryan asked, as the server brought their entrées.

"It's as if the person who writes these is fluent in English but pretending not to be," Aidan said. "Maybe an American, maybe a foreign diplomat or business executive who wants us to believe these are coming from someone with only basic literacy."

"The lack of consistency is a pattern itself," Ashley said. "The writer is making deliberate errors but isn't making the same ones twice, so that means he or she is trying to confuse you."

As they ate, the six of them debated and discussed the similarity between the email messages to Ricardo and the bomb threat, and by the time the meal was over they had all agreed Ricardo had to go to the police. "Even if the threat to you is over, there's someone dangerous out there, and you have to do what you can to stop him or her," Ashley said.

Ricardo reluctantly agreed. When they finished eating, Ashley left to return to the convention center for the afternoon session and Ryan said he thought he'd try his luck at the casino. "Call or text if you need anything," he said to Liam as he left.

Liam relaxed, for the first time in days. Their personal waiting game was over, and Ricardo had released the results of his research to the world. Now it was up to the world to do something about it.

20 – Families

"I am not ready to go to the police yet," Ricardo said. "I need to relax and center myself first." He looked at Blake. "And no, I do not need the crystals or anything else to help me. Just a walk, somewhere quiet or interesting."

"There are a lot of parts of the hotel we haven't explored yet," Aidan said. "There's an area they call the Dig, fake architectural ruins that surround the pool. It might be nice to go over there."

Aidan pulled up a map of the complex on his phone. "We have to go through the casino first, and then the predator lagoon. Will you be all right walking past some sharks?"

"Man is the apex predator on this planet," Ricardo said. "If I am no longer afraid of men, then I will not worry about sharks, either."

Aidan smiled. It was a nice thought, but at least the sharks were in a controlled environment.

The casino was bright and noisy, and Aidan kept expecting Ricardo to react, to get twitchy or retreat into himself, but he seemed to enjoy the bells and whistles and flashing lights. "I feel like today is a lucky day," he said, as he stopped in front of a slot machine with a jungle theme.

He pulled a ten-dollar bill from his wallet and fed it into the slot, then chose to bet the maximum. He pulled the lever at the machine's side, and the symbols began rolling down the screen. Jungle woman, jungle woman, wild card, jungle woman, wild card.

Ricardo's face lit up with enjoyment like a little kid with a lollipop as the numbers multiplied on the screen. "See, I told you I am lucky today." He pressed the cash out button, and ticket spit out showing he'd won fifty dollars on his ten-dollar bet. "We will cash this out later. Now, we continue."

Aidan felt that at last he was seeing Ricardo's true character, and his take-charge attitude clearly had to be tumultuous mixed with Blake's. Blake seemed on edge, as if he was sure that Ricardo's craziness would manifest again. Aidan had no idea how things would play out, now that the threat had been removed. He was merely an interested bystander.

There was a possibility that their antagonist might seek revenge, but if Aidan was correct, then the man who had made all the threats was only interested in stopping Ricardo from speaking. Now, he was probably scrambling to deal with the effects of the information becoming public.

They left the casino and entered a glass tunnel surrounded by water. It led along the bottom of the lagoon where the sharks and other predators swam around them. It was a weird sensation, as if they were the ones on display instead of the fish, and Aidan worried that Ricardo would freak out once more. But instead he chatted happily, pointing out nurse sharks and hammerheads, admiring the way they glided so effortlessly through the water.

"Wasn't it a Woody Allen movie that said something about sharks?" Aidan asked. "The way they have to keep moving?"

"*Annie Hall*," Blake said. "Alvy Singer said that his relationship with Annie was like a dead shark because it had stopped moving."

Ricardo reached over and took Blake's hand. "Our relationship continues to move, *mi amor*," he said. "No dead sharks for us."

Aidan's heart was warmed by the smile they shared. He wanted to reach for Liam's hand, too, but they were still working, and would be until they delivered Ricardo safely back to Philadelphia.

They climbed up a winding staircase to a bar in the middle of the lagoon. The building was intricately designed with seashells on the roof and in the railings, and reminded Aidan of a Gaudi church—this one worshipping tropical vacations.

They ordered colorful drinks—virgin piña coladas for Aidan and Liam, alcoholic ones for Ricardo and Blake. Then they walked through a swinging rope bridge to the jungle-like area surrounding the various pools. They got wristbands at a towel hut and strolled under a canopy of palm trees.

"I want to thank you all, Blake especially, for putting up with me while I was under the influence of those awful medications," Ricardo said. It was cool and moist under there, so different from the blazing sun. Like a sheltered moment in time.

"I am glad you are better, sweetheart," Blake said.

"So are we," Aidan said. "Though it's a lot easier to protect you now that you're calmer."

They left the shelter of the palms for a slippery wooden deck around one of the saltwater pools. Tiny children gathered at the shallow end in brightly colored water wings, while mothers and fathers hovered nearby. At the deeper end, a boy cannonballed into the water with a mighty splash. In the distance Aidan saw the tower of the Mayan pool slide, heard the laughter of parents and kids sliding down it and splashing in the pool.

It was the perfect place for a family vacation, Aidan thought. Too bad he and Liam would never have children. As an only child, he had no nieces or nephews, just the children of his cousins. Living in Tunisia, and then France, had kept his role in their lives to the briefest of visits.

Liam had two sisters and a niece and nephew, but relations with his family were rough, and had been long before he came out. His late father had been abusive, and his elderly mother was a foul-mouthed biddy. Liam's sisters resented the way he had deserted them to enlist in the Navy, and he had only sporadic contact with them, usually responding to emails about their kids.

We all make choices, Aidan thought, as they moved from the wooden deck to a sandy beach by the Atlantic. If he and Liam were younger, and ensconced in more traditional careers, they might have chosen to adopt, or have a baby by surrogate. So many younger couples were doing that.

It wasn't too late, of course. Both of them still had presumably viable sperm, and if they gave up close protection entirely they would have more time to devote to family life. But Aidan didn't see that in the cards for the future. Too bad they hadn't asked the Rastafarian at the crystal shop if he could read the Tarot for them.

Blake stumbled in the sand, and Ricardo grabbed his arm and steadied him. Blake's dress shirt was soaked with sweat by that point and he looked miserable, yet determined to continue the walk if it made his husband happy.

Ricardo said, "I believe I am ready to speak with the police. There needs to be justice for the victims of the bombing, and their families, and I must provide whatever evidence I have to make that happen."

21 – Interrogations

Aidan led the way as they returned to the suite. While Blake showered, Liam called the front desk and asked if they could send Shadrach up to speak with them.

Ricardo was nervous, pacing around the living room. When Liam hung up the phone, he said, "Ricardo. Sit. You're making us all nervous."

"What if the police do not believe me? Suppose they think I sent the threats myself?"

"Why would you interrupt your own session?" Liam said. "I've spoken to Shadrach and he seems like a smart guy. He'll listen to us and tell us what to do."

"But this is a simple island. There is probably little the police can do anyway."

A few minutes later Shadrach knocked on the door, and Aidan let him in. Though it was only early afternoon, he looked exhausted, and there were sweat pockets under the arms of his polo shirt. *A bomb threat at your hotel could wear you down*, Liam thought.

"You wanted to speak with me?" Shadrach asked.

Liam motioned him to the table. "We have some information that we believe connects to the bomb threat this morning."

The exhaustion in Shadrach's face disappeared and he looked very alert. "Please tell me."

Blake joined them, and the five of them sat at the table. Liam took the lead in explaining the threats that Ricardo had received, both in Philadelphia and then in the Bahamas. "You should have reported these threats to us when you arrived," Shadrach said, and the lilt in his voice became harsher. "We would have been better prepared to protect the conference."

"Aidan and I weren't aware of the full extent of the threats when we began this assignment," Liam said. "We only learned information in bits and pieces, and then had to put them together." He showed the security chief the texts he had, and then compared them to the bomb threat.

Aidan took over then. "You can see that there are similarities between the way the email threats are written, and the wording in the bomb threat," he said. "My expertise is in teaching English to foreign language students, and I can tell you that someone who speaks good English has been trying to make the email threats to Mr. Levy, and the bomb threat to the hotel, look like they were written by someone with limited English skills. The writer makes different kinds of errors in each message, and rarely repeats the same mistake. A real writer struggling with English wouldn't write that way."

Shadrach ignored Aidan and turned to Liam. "How did you get this message?" he demanded. "Only the police should have access to this."

"A friend got it for us," Liam said. "Do you see the connections we are making?"

"What I see is that you have gained access to protected police materials. That is a very serious problem in our country."

"You make it sound like we've done something wrong," Blake said indignantly. "We're trying to help you find the person who threatened your hotel. Don't you care about that?"

"I care about many things," Shadrach said. "I care about the security of our hotel and our guests. But also about the security of my country."

He frowned. "I will have to speak with someone I know in the police administration. He will not be happy that you have accessed this bomb threat. He may be too suspicious of you to take your information seriously."

Aidan was surprised that Shadrach didn't shuffle them off to the cops, but maybe he was more concerned with protecting the resort.

Shadrach pushed his chair back and stood up. "How much longer will you be staying?"

"The conference ends tomorrow morning," Ricardo said. "We fly back to Philadelphia in the afternoon."

"Then I will have to speak with the police officer investigating the bombings now." He stepped out onto the balcony, closed the door behind him, and pulled out his cell phone.

Ricardo looked at Liam. "What do you think will happen now?"

"Hard to say yet. Whether they believe you or not, we're still scheduled to leave tomorrow."

"What if they try to prevent us from leaving?" Blake asked. "Will we need a lawyer here?"

"Let's see what Shadrach says," Liam said.

Shadrach came back into the suite from the balcony. He looked angry, though Liam couldn't tell if the anger was directed at them, or at the policeman he had spoken with.

"Inspector Pickett would like to speak with you but he is not free until four o'clock. He will come to the hotel then and I will bring him up here."

"That would be fine," Liam said. "Thank you for your help."

After Shadrach left, Aidan looked at his watch. "We completely forgot about the rest of the afternoon sessions. The last session for today begins in about ten minutes. Did you want to go to that, Ricardo?"

He pursed his lips. "Yes, I have come all this way. I should hear what all my colleagues have to say."

Security had returned to its original level, and Aidan was able to use his guest pass to accompany Ricardo inside the auditorium.

Another of the academic women Aidan had noticed presented in the last session of the afternoon, about how Sephardic Jews from Morocco had emigrated to Peru in the early part of the 19th century, where they settled in the Amazon basin and worked as traders and trappers.

Aidan found it hard to imagine members of his family, who were all college graduates who worked in business, education or similar fields, out in the Amazon basin hunting down jaguars and skinning them to sell the pelts. But that belied his own prejudices about Jews as smart People of the Book. It was good to listen to speeches like this that opened his eyes to the different kinds of Jews in the world.

"Do you think that your material will reach the wider audience you want?" Aidan asked Ricardo as they walked out.

"I hope so. I have devoted years of my life to this project. I want it to be worthwhile."

He looked at Aidan. "And you? How do you find value in your life? Is it in the people you protect?"

"I want to do good in the world," Aidan said, surprising himself. "Sometimes that is in a very small way, like when I was teaching and I saw a student learn some complicated concept in English grammar or punctuation. Working with Liam, I have had the opportunity to save lives and to see romances blossom where none seemed possible."

"You are a good man, Mr. Greene," Ricardo said. "I appreciate everything you and your husband have done to protect me and help me get my message out."

"What will you do now?"

"Now? I return to Philadelphia, and to my work at the Institute. I have new ideas for research, and the speakers here have spurred my interest in collaboration as well."

They met up with Liam and returned to the suite. At a few minutes past four, Shadrach and Inspector Pickett arrived. Pickett was an older man with a desiccated look, and his skin was several shades lighter than Shadrach's rich ebony.

"Shadrach tells me that you have shown him a copy of the bomb threat that the hotel received," he said. "Did one of you send it?"

Aidan was glad that Liam took charge of the conversation. He would have been too tempted to say something sarcastic.

"None of us would have any reason to disrupt the conference,"

Liam said. "My partner and I were hired by Mr. Chennault to protect Mr. Levy while he is here."

"Ah, yes, protect. From threats he says he received."

"I showed Shadrach the threats earlier this afternoon." Liam reached for his phone. "I can show them to you as well. You'll see that…"

"That is not necessary," Pickett interrupted. "If you did not send the threat, then you must have illegally obtained access to it. Would you please tell me how you got this document?"

"We have contacts within the United States diplomatic service who were able to secure a copy for us from the Bahamian police. I am not at liberty to reveal them, but I am sure if you speak with people inside your office you will discover who passed on the threat to the U.S. government."

"You have an answer for everything," Pickett said.

"Because I am telling you the truth," Liam said. "My clients, my partner and I have nothing to hide. We are simply trying to help the police with your inquiries. Because of the similarities between the threats…"

Once again, Pickett interrupted. "Which are nonsense. Shadrach forwarded your so-called threats to me, and I looked at the materials myself. There is no similarity to the wording."

"It's not the wording, it's the way that the author is trying to cover up his knowledge of English," Aidan protested.

"You are not police," Pickett said forcefully. "You must not meddle in my investigation, or I will have you arrested and jailed here in my country."

With a loud scraping noise, he pushed back his chair and stood up. "Good day, gentlemen. I trust we will have no reason to speak again."

Shadrach followed him out, and Aidan realized the hotel security chief hadn't said a word, either in their defense or to state his own opinion.

"Well," Aidan said after they were gone, the door to the suite closing carefully behind them. "Where does that leave us?"

"We did what we had to do," Liam said. "We gave the police information in our possession that might have a bearing on their investigation into the bomb threat. That's all we were obligated to do."

"I told you they would do nothing," Ricardo said.

"What if the police come back?" Blake asked.

Liam shrugged. "We have done nothing wrong, so there is no reason for them to charge us and create an international incident."

The four of them decided to return to the first restaurant they had tried, one of those run by a celebrity chef. As they reached the glamorous entrance, all hanging icicles and elaborate drapes, Ethan Silverberg once again approached from the shadows, as if that was his typical *modus operandi*. Aidan thought that if he was trying to sabotage politicians for his blog, that was probably a good move. However, with Liam still in full protection mode, it wasn't as effective.

Liam stepped in front of Silverberg for long enough to make his point, then stepped aside so he could speak with Ricardo.

"I posted the text of your speech on my blog this afternoon," Silverberg said. "I took photos of the slides where you provided the proof behind your assertions, and added them, too. Since then, the traffic counter on my site has gone wild."

As if to underscore what he said, in the background a couple of little kids in strollers started to cry and scream.

"What do you mean, wild?" Ricardo asked.

Blake, Liam and Aidan clustered around to hear the answer.

Silverberg beamed. "Hundreds of distinct visitors, and lots of referral links. I checked to see where the traffic is coming from, and my three top countries are the United States, Argentina, and Iran."

"Iran?" Ricardo asked, his voice sounding strangled. "It is one of the worst countries in the world for internet freedom." Behind them, the long draperies swayed as the air conditioning kicked in.

Silverberg nodded. "Which means most of the people coming to the blog are doing so either from government connections, or cell phones." He turned to the three of them. "As Mr. Levy may have told you, in repressive regimes like the one in Tehran, anti-government activists must use their cell phones to access the internet."

"What does this mean, in real terms?" Aidan asked.

"It means that Washington, Buenos Aires and Tehran are paying attention to my information," Ricardo said. "Whether that is good or bad remains to be seen."

22 – Trust

Aidan was interested in the way that Silverberg seamlessly integrated himself into the group after Ricardo invited the blogger to join them, then introduced Blake as his husband, and Liam and Aidan as his bodyguards.

The five of them sat at a round table, Liam facing the front entrance and Aidan the kitchen door. They couldn't assume that Ricardo was safe until they returned him to Philadelphia.

"I am not surprised that you chose to hire personal security," Silverberg said to Ricardo as they settled at the table. "The information you presented was quite explosive."

"I received numerous threats against my life," Ricardo said. "But I was determined to appear at the conference and make sure that this evidence came to light."

"I would like to point out that Mr. Silverberg represents the media," Blake said. "And that anything any of us say this evening might show up on his blog."

Silverberg smiled. "Yes, you're an attorney, aren't you, Blake?"

"And a devoted husband. I don't want anyone else to get ideas about harming Ricardo."

"Understood. I promise you that anything I learn this evening will not make it online without express permission."

That seemed to relax Blake, though Aidan was still uncertain if Silverberg could be trusted. He noted that Blake steered the conversation away from the threats Ricardo had received to Ricardo's work at the Institute. Silverberg listened intently, even though in Aidan's opinion nothing Ricardo was working on was as explosive as the AMIA bombing revelations.

As they ate their entrées, Silverberg turned his attention to Aidan and Liam. "I'm sure that much of your work is confidential, but I wonder if you could speak in general terms about the kind of clients you represent, and what you do to keep them safe."

Liam looked to Aidan and nodded slightly.

"We work for a French company called the Agence de Securité," Aidan said. "Most of the work is boring—we accompany clients to meetings, we assess the surroundings for threats, and so on."

"That's why I've seen your husband outside the conference auditorium," Silverberg said, nodding. "And I saw you with Ricardo during the meetings. I assume you chose your seats with an eye to a quick exit in case of trouble."

He asked a couple of additional questions about the kinds of clients who employed them, which Aidan dodged.

"And then there was the bomb threat." Silverberg leaned in close. "Do you think that threat was related to Ricardo's speech? It came in right before he was to speak."

"Proximity is not necessarily an indicator of cause," Aidan said. "In our business it's best not to make too many assumptions."

Silverberg danced around the issue for a few minutes, but no one was willing to answer his questions. Eventually, he gave up and he and Ricardo gossiped about some of the other speakers and their papers.

Silverberg invited them to the bar for cocktails after dinner, and Aidan was relieved when Ricardo declined and they bid goodnight to Silverberg. After Liam had checked out the suite, they all went inside, and quickly retired to their respective bedrooms.

"Long day," Aidan said, collapsing on the bed.

"I agree. I could have kicked Ricardo when he invited that internet geek to have dinner with us."

"Yeah, I don't trust him, but you know the saying. Keep your friends close and your enemies closer."

"You think he's our enemy?" Liam asked.

Aidan kicked off his deck shoes, feeling the rough carpet beneath his toes. "Only in the sense that he has access to a worldwide platform, and it would be very easy for him to take the simplest piece of information and blow it out of proportion. I'm worried that he might follow up on his piece about Ricardo with a second article about him hiring bodyguards because his presentation was so threatening. I think it's great that he is getting Ricardo's material worldwide attention, but I don't want him to do anything to put Ricardo in the way of further harm."

"Spoken like a true bodyguard," Liam said. "You have learned much, grasshopper."

"And as you get older, you look more and more like Master Po," Aidan said. "I think you might even be developing a bald spot."

Reflexively, Liam raised his hand to his head. "You're evil," he said, with a laugh.

"Oh, really? Do you need to punish me? Or reward me for

speaking 'like a true bodyguard'?"

Liam smiled. "We can work that out as we go." He moved over to Aidan and pulled the hem of Aidan's polo shirt out of his slacks. He slid his hands up beneath the fabric to find Aidan's nipples and squeeze them.

"Oh," Aidan moaned.

They heard a bang from the next bedroom, and both of them tensed. When the bang was repeated, Aidan said, "That sounds like the bed frame hitting the wall."

They listened again, and the third time Liam agreed. "Our client is busy with his husband. Which gives us the freedom to get busy together."

He leaned down and kissed Aidan and tweaked his nipples once more. Aidan's dick stiffened, and he unbuckled his belt, undid his pants, and let them slip to the floor. His dick pushed his boxers forward.

As Liam deepened the kiss, pulling his arms out from under the fabric of Aidan's shirt to wrap around his back, Aidan undid Liam's pants as well. He was happy to feel that Liam's dick was as hard as his own, pulsing against his jock strap.

They kissed, and then Aidan stepped back and pulled off his polo shirt, and Liam did the same. "Does it turn you on knowing your ex is getting fucked in the next room?" Liam asked.

"We don't know that Ricardo is topping Blake," Aidan said.

"That's right, you said he thought anything to do with the ass was dirty." Liam shook his head. "What a fool." He smiled. "But Ricardo's bigger than he is. Maybe the Latin lover is taking charge, throwing his husband down on the bed and fucking the life out of him."

"Now you're getting creepy," Aidan said, though his dick did seem to prong more stiffly at the thought of stuck-up Blake Chennault taking it up the ass—and loving it.

"I like the sound of that," Aidan continued. "Throwing my husband on the bed and fucking the life of out of him."

"Only you don't have to throw me." Liam pulled off his polo shirt and dropped his jock strap to the floor. His meaty dick flapped against his stomach. "I'll go there willingly."

"I'll bet you will." Aidan followed Liam's lead, and by the time he was naked Liam was lying on the bed, his legs spread, his eyes glazed with lust. Very slowly, he lifted his legs, exposing his pink hole, surrounded by dark hairs.

"I can get into that." Aidan grabbed the bottle of lube from the bedside table and squeezed some onto the fingers of his right hand. Then he knelt on the bed and began exploring.

There was something so erotic about a big, masculine man like Liam opening himself up to be penetrated. Aidan couldn't imagine Blake ever assuming such a position—even though it was possible he was doing so at that moment. The occasional banging of the headboard against the wall continued, interspersed with periods of quiet when Aidan imagined Ricardo stopping to suck Blake's dick.

Oh, God. There he was again, imagining Blake's dick while he was in the middle of sex with Liam. He turned his full attention to his husband's ass, threading his index finger up and in, searching for Liam's prostate. He knew he'd reached it when Liam moaned with pleasure.

Aidan pushed a second finger in, teased Liam for a while, then pulled out. He squeezed more lube on his dick and then scooted up close to Liam, his husband's tree-trunk thighs pressed against his chest, and made his entrance, slow at first to make sure Liam was comfortable. Only when Liam pulled him closer and said, "More, harder, faster," did he pick up the tempo.

"Bang that headboard," Liam said. "Make your ex wonder who's fucking who now."

They'd always talked dirty to one another, but this conversation pushed Aidan farther, until he lost all control and was bucking Liam's ass like a rodeo cowboy, rising his ass from the bed, pushing down, forcing the headboard against the wall.

He couldn't even give Liam a warning, he was so lost in the moment. He shot his load up his husband's ass with a passion that shook through his entire body. It was only when he opened his eyes and looked down that he saw Liam had come as well.

"I didn't even touch you," Aidan said.

"You didn't have to. I love you so much." There was a light dancing in Liam's eyes.

"You were thinking of Blake and Ricardo, weren't you?" Aidan demanded.

"Not Ricardo. I admit I did have a brief fantasy of Blake standing behind you, fucking you as you plunged into me."

Aidan slumped down beside him. "Naughty boy. That is so not happening."

"You never know. We have another day together tomorrow."

Aidan snuggled into his side. "I trust that when the time comes that I'm not enough for you, you'll let me know."

Liam leaned down and kissed the top of his head. "Not going to happen, husband."

* * *

Friday morning, Aidan woke early and began packing as Liam exercised out on the balcony. When his husband came in, Aidan said, "Do you want to get some laps in at the pool here? You won't have this kind of facility when we get back home."

Liam smiled. "You think I didn't get enough of a workout last night?"

"I want you to maintain that magnificent physique of yours."

"Well, if it's for you." He leaned over and kissed Aidan on the lips. Then he put on his flip-flops and a T-shirt and walked out of the bedroom.

Aidan heard him speak briefly to Blake, before Liam went out the door. Aidan finished packing and walked out to the living room, where Blake sat with a copy of the *New York Times*.

"Where did you get that?" Aidan asked. "Have you been having it delivered to the suite this week?"

Blake shook his head. "I was Googling Ricardo this morning and a link came up that mentioned a *Times* article. I went down to the lobby to get it. Do you know how busy this hotel is at six in the morning?"

"Probably lots of people heading out to flights or wanting to get an early shot at day trips. Anything interesting in the article?"

"A reporter picked up Ethan Silverberg's feed and tried to get comments from government officials in Buenos Aires. Nothing major, but it does look like Ricardo's information has reached the mainstream."

They talked for a few more minutes, about their arrangements to leave that evening for the flight to Philadelphia, and then Ricardo appeared. Liam was still down at the pool, but Aidan felt that with Ricardo's information out there in the world, he could manage the client on his own.

Ricardo and Aidan went downstairs and took their regular seats in the auditorium. The last speaker was a former ambassador from Mexico to Israel, and he spoke in grand terms about the need to continue to build relationships between Latin America and Israel, primarily when it came to trade, though also as a way to keep Jews in the Diaspora connected to the Holy Land.

The conference organizers took the stage after the presentation, to thank everyone for attending. "Audio CDs will be available for order from the conference website within the week," he announced. "And the text of all the speeches would all be published in the *Journal of International Jewish Relations* in the spring issue."

Ricardo turned to Aidan and whispered, "Last night Blake and I had international Jewish relations."

Aidan couldn't help laughing. "We heard."

"It was the first time in many months." He smiled.

The audience applauded when the speaker called the conference closed, and Aidan and Ricardo walked outside.

"Why didn't you tell me you were coming to the conference this morning?" he demanded. "I was swimming and I ran into Ryan Wood. When he told me Ashley was here, I jumped out of the pool and called the room. Blake told me you were here. You shouldn't have come without telling me."

Ricardo looked abashed, though maybe he was embarrassed at the way Liam was dripping on the carpet.

"Calm down, sweetheart," Aidan said. "The threat is over, remember? Ricardo has released all his information, it's gone online, and Blake showed me a mention in the *New York Times* this morning. There was no reason for us to wait for you. I am perfectly capable of accompanying a client, you know."

"I know. But we should be making joint decisions, even if we feel the threat has lifted." He frowned. "And I know it's my fault, too. I should have asked if Ricardo was going to the session this morning before I went swimming."

He turned to head toward the elevator, providing Aidan with an excellent view of his wet shorts hugging his ass. Ricardo must have seen it, too, because he raised his eyebrows at Aidan and smiled.

23 – Lazy River

Liam was irritated. He had let his guard down, and even though nothing awful had happened, it was still a lapse in attention. He wanted to blame Aidan, but it was his own fault. He dodged around a little boy with a giant inflatable shark, only to find himself behind a pair of plus-sized Bahamian women who were both engaged in separate phone calls and moving slowly down the hallway to the elevators.

He was glad to get up to the suite, strip off his wet T-shirt and shorts, and jump into a long, hot shower. He focused on his breathing, willing himself to relax. By the time he was ready to dress in his regular clothes, he felt more in control of his emotions.

When he came out to the living room, he found Aidan, Blake and Ricardo sitting at the round table. Ricardo said, "I want to do something fun now that I can relax fully. What is the lazy river? I heard people speaking about it this morning."

Oh, no, Liam thought. *Not another way to put the client in danger.*

"It's a manufactured stream that curves around through part of the property," Aidan said. "There are machines in the wall that create a current, and you get into an inner tube and ride along."

"It sounds like a ride for children," Blake said.

"I've looked out at it from the balcony," Aidan said. ""Lots of adults use it. It looks very relaxing. Let me show you." He walked over to the balcony and opened the sliding door, then stepped outside with

Ricardo.

Liam wanted to grab him and shake him. Why was he encouraging this kind of behavior when they were so close to finishing this assignment and going home?

Liam turned to Blake. "When we get you and Ricardo to Philadelphia this evening, I assume our assignment will be complete?"

Blake nodded. "It's miraculous the way that Ricardo has bounced back from those medications. I didn't realize that it was the pills causing the delusions, but after he stopped I did some reading and realized that in some cases if the underlying problem goes away, the medication can continue the symptoms. I assume that's what's been going on, but either way I'm relieved he's better. You'll have the company you work for send me the bill?"

"I will."

Ricardo and Aidan came back in. "The lazy river looks wonderful. I want to go there and relax," Ricardo said.

"I don't think that's a good idea," Liam said. "It's a very vulnerable area and would be difficult to protect you."

"I don't need protection anymore," Ricardo said. "We have only a few hours left here, and I would like to make it a holiday."

Liam turned to Blake. "Please? Can we choose something else? There's a secluded private pool at one of the other towers. We could go swimming there."

"I want to try the lazy river," Ricardo insisted. "I will take full responsibility for anything that happens there."

"If it's what my husband wants, then I have to go along with him,"

Blake said.

Liam looked at Aidan, who seemed to be unwilling to jump into the argument. "Fine," Liam said. "But if there's any hint of trouble, you listen to me immediately."

"Yes, sir," Ricardo said, and he saluted.

"Now that he's not crazy, Ricardo's a handful," Liam said when he and Aidan were alone in their room, putting on fresh T-shirts and swimsuits. Liam was glad that Aidan had packed two suits for each of them. He hated having to slide a cold, wet suit back on.

Another way in which he'd gotten soft since his years in the military. He wouldn't have thought to complain about being ordered back into a suit for another long hard swim when he was a SEAL, often carrying twenty or thirty pounds on his back. Now he was complaining about a river ride that would do all the work for him.

He hated to compromise on anything involving safety for the client. Yes, Ricardo's information was public, which theoretically removed the threat against him. But as Ethan Silverberg had pointed out, government officials in Argentina and Iran were reading Silverberg's blog post, and that could make people in power in those countries very unhappy.

Liam was still alert as they walked down to the elevator together. He was surprised that Ricardo was willing to jump into a car with a mother, father and two kids in strollers, but he followed the client's lead.

Everyone they passed as they threaded their way through the hotel and out to the entrance to the lazy river looked happy, relaxed and on vacation. Maybe Ricardo was right. The threat had passed, and they'd all earned the chance to relax.

Birds chirped in the trees above them, and the fronds of a palm bounced as a squirrel jumped from one tree to another. Under the tree cover it was warm, but not uncomfortably hot, and a gentle breeze floated through from the ocean.

They walked down a curving stone path to the start of the lazy river ride. There were two kinds of inner tubes you could ride in—single ones and double ones. An older couple nearly spilled over trying to get out of their double, and Liam stepped into the thigh-high water, grabbed hold of it and steadied it so they could get out.

He held onto the raft as the cool water splashed his groin, and Ricardo got in the front, letting his legs hang out. The float swirled gently in the current, and Blake clambered in the other side, as if he was riding pillion on a motorcycle.

Ricardo kicked his legs and the raft took off down the river. Liam grabbed a single inner tube as it came past and held it out for Aidan. His poor husband was comical in his effort to get in and settle down. He nearly tipped over as he tried to get his legs over the outer edge of the tube, resting his butt in the center.

Liam laughed. "You try and get in this without looking like a fool," Aidan said. A kid upstream jumped out of another single tube, and Aidan grabbed it as it floated past.

Liam lifted his right leg high, higher than was comfortable, and managed to step into the center of the tube easily. With Aidan still holding it, he got his left leg in as well, then sat back, letting his legs dangle through the opening.

The gentle sound of a reggae beat drifted through the trees as Liam kicked off, then sat back against the plastic. By then, Ricardo and Blake were already around the next corner, and Liam alternately kicked and paddled with the flat of his hands to catch up.

Ricardo and Blake were laughing as they bounced against a cluster of tubes caught at a sharp turn. They looked so happy, and Liam thought that was the greatest benefit of working in close protection. Seeing clients relax and enjoy life.

The threat wasn't past yet, though. He continued to monitor their progress, and the movement of staff members through the trees, who moved along making sure everyone in the river was paying attention to the rules.

The current kept them moving at a relaxing pace, and Liam began thinking about how good a cold, frothy tropical drink would taste once they finished. The four of them stayed in close contact as they meandered, bounced against walls, steered around families, and let the water drift them forward.

By Liam's estimation, they were about halfway around the circular track when the shots rang out.

24 – Undressed

To Aidan, it looked like a giant hand had pushed Ricardo against the back of the tube. It was only once the float begin to deflate that he heard shots, due to the curious property of the travel of sound. Liam leapt out of his float with surprising grace and grabbed the double float, while Aidan struggled to get out of his, then gave up and simply pushed himself over there.

A woman screamed, which incited children to scream, too, and the lazy river backed up as families and couples floating behind them came to rest. Ricardo lolled back in the sinking float as Liam tried to lift him out. "What happened?" Blake asked. "What's going on?"

A river attendant in shorts and a hotel-logo T-shirt materialized out of the woods and jumped into the water, though he was more interested in getting the double raft pushed to the side and out of the way of the people behind. It was only when he looked down and saw Ricardo's blood washing onto his white T-shirt that he blanched and blew a whistle.

"Call an ambulance!" Liam told him, but the boy didn't have a radio, and they had to wait an extra minute for a security guard to arrive. He and Liam managed to lift Ricardo out of the water and lay him on the ground.

People were screaming and flailing around in their rafts, and Aidan had trouble getting out of his and onto the ground. He grabbed Blake's hand and tugged him up to the other edge of the river. While they waited for the traffic to pass, he told Blake to hold onto the wall, and Aidan managed to step out of his raft.

Then he helped Blake out, and the two of them waded across the river to the other side, where Liam helped them both climb out. Ricardo had already lost a lot of blood by the time the security guard had fashioned a tourniquet over the wound in his stomach.

More guards had appeared by then, closing the river ride, moving everyone away, and using their radios to direct an ambulance crew. Though it was hot, Blake was shivering, and Aidan wrapped his arm around Blake's shoulders. The reggae music in the background abruptly stopped, as did the movement of the water in the lazy river. Unfortunately the lack of sound magnified the cries of women and small children, and Aidan wanted to yell at them all to shut up.

No matter how hard he and Liam had tried, they had made a crucial mistake in allowing the client to be vulnerable, and they had failed in their duty to keep Ricardo safe.

After what seemed like an hour, but was probably only fifteen minutes, the ambulance crew came pushing through the undergrowth with a stretcher. They rested it on a flat space and carefully lifted Ricardo onto it. He was grimacing, moaning with pain.

Aidan felt like his heart was ripped open. Ricardo was even more than their client; he had become a friend as well, and Aidan felt an extra closeness to him because of their shared connection to Blake.

Blake looked almost as if he'd been shot as well. His pupils were enlarged, his skin cold and clammy, and he looked abnormally pale.

The EMTs leaned down and each took one end of the stretcher, then stood up carefully. "I'll go with him," Blake announced. "He's my husband."

The lead EMT looked skeptical, and Aidan remembered reading that same-sex marriage was not legal in the Bahamas. He worried that Blake would run into trouble at the hospital – but if there was anyone who could take control of such a situation, it was Blake Chennault.

"We'll be right behind you." Liam turned to the EMT. "Where are you taking him?"

"Princess Margaret Hospital," the man replied in a gentle accent. "On Shirley Street in downtown Nassau. Any taxi driver can take you."

Blake cast one last, stricken look at them, like Lot's wife leaving Sodom, then turned to follow the two EMTs as they fought their way through the underbrush.

"Should we go after them?" Aidan asked.

Liam shook his head. "There's a walkway over on the other side of the river. We can make better time if we cross back over and take that." He jumped into the water and held his hand out for Aidan, who ignored it and jumped in on his own.

"We screwed up," Liam said, as they pushed their way through the still water to the other side. "Let our guard down. And this is what happens."

"It's always a balancing act. Ricardo thought that once he gave his speech, he'd be safe, and we tried to accommodate him," Aidan said. "We made a mistake. But we can't dwell on that right now. We need dry clothes, and a change for Blake, too."

They made it to the other side, and Liam put his hands on the stone wall and vaulted up. This time Aidan took his hand, and Liam hauled him up until he could get his feet on the stone. "How do you think he looked?" Aidan asked, as they took off down the path.

"He lost a lot of blood," Liam said. "Only the doctor can say if the bullet hit any organs."

As they hurried into the hotel, Aidan noticed the way several people looked at the blood on Liam's T-shirt and gave them a wide berth. Once in the suite, Liam jumped into the shower to wash the blood off his arms and legs.

Aidan dried himself and changed into the clothes he'd worn earlier in the day, leaving out a clean jockstrap, polo shirt and slacks for Liam. Then he went into the other bedroom, where he grabbed a pair of slacks and a business shirt for Blake. He knew his ex would want to look as professional as possible if he had to argue with the hospital, so he threw in a pair of black socks and Blake's wing-tips.

At the last minute he realized Blake would need underwear too, and went into his drawer for a pair of boxers. He was surprised to find none—only bikini briefs.

And a dildo.

My, my, how things have changed, Aidan thought. The Blake he knew and lived with would never have worn such skimpy underwear—and he'd disdained all sex toys then, too.

"Come on, we need to get moving," Liam called from the living room.

"I'm packing." Aidan folded Blake's clothes carefully and put them into his ex's bag. At the last minute, he hurried into the bathroom and took one of the big white towels too.

"Why are you taking so much?" Liam demanded.

"Because I know Blake. And I know that the Bahamas doesn't always recognize same-sex marriages, and if Ricardo gets the wrong doctor or nurse Blake may not be able to make the necessary medical decisions. I know Blake, and he needs to be dressed properly in order to argue effectively."

Aidan noticed that Liam must have cut his lower arm somewhere. He had wrapped one of the white towels around it to staunch the blood.

"What happened to your arm?"

"Nothing major. I can get it looked at when we get to the hospital. Come on."

Despite his husband's reassurance, Aidan was worried. The burglar had stolen their first aid kit, so he had nothing to treat Liam's wound with. When was the last time they'd had their tetanus shots? What if the cut wasn't a scrape, but ran deeper?

Liam hurried out the door. Aidan made sure it locked behind him and trundled the bag behind Liam to the elevator.

"Spin me a story," Liam said, as they waited. An old episode of *MacGyver* played on the TV there, Richard Dean Anderson figuring his way out of another tough situation. "Why would someone want to kill Ricardo after he's already made his proof public?"

"Anger? Revenge?"

"We've been thinking this case is about international politics,"

Liam said. "Those motives don't matter to politicians. They're too busy doing damage control."

"At the international level," Aidan said. "But what if someone's job was to keep this information from getting out, and he's screwed up by letting it happen? He may be facing sanctions by the government. He could lose his job and his family could suffer. That could lead to anger and revenge."

The elevator door opened, and they squeezed in with a group of Japanese businessmen, some older, some younger. One of the older men spoke urgently, while the others agreed at intervals, speaking loudly and bobbing their heads in abbreviated bows.

Liam led the way to the lobby, then out to the taxi ranks. He headed to the front of the line, where he unwrapped his arm and said, "Need to go to the hospital now."

The people at the head of the line stepped back, and Aidan and Liam hopped into the rear of the first taxi. "Princess Margaret Hospital, emergency room," Liam said.

The interior of the cab was hot and humid, and Aidan began to sweat. He leaned forward. "Can you turn on the air conditioning?"

"She broke," the driver said. "But we cool down as we move." The cab did cool a bit as they went through the tunnel, and then again when they were crossing the bridge back to Nassau. There was heavy traffic once they got on local roads again. Aidan imagined how Blake must have felt, riding in the ambulance beside Ricardo.

Aidan had had a bad scare when Liam broke his arm, but nothing like this. Would Ricardo live? How serious was his wound? Would he need an air ambulance back to the States?

Liam must have known what he was thinking about because he said, "We can't do anything until we get to the hospital and see how he's doing. Try to relax, so we can be on our game if we need to be."

They paid the cab driver and rushed through the Emergency Room entrance at Princess Margaret Hospital. Blake was sitting on a hard plastic chair in the waiting room, still soaking wet. He seemed to be in shock. "How's Ricardo?" Liam asked.

"Waiting to go to the operating room. All they'll tell me is that the bullet nicked his spleen and they need to do some repair. He's lost a lot of blood."

"Come with me," Aidan said, tugging on Blake's hand. "Let's go to the men's room and get you changed."

"I'll see what I can find out," Liam said.

Aidan led Blake to a single-unit men's room, followed him inside and locked the door. "Wet clothes off," Aidan said.

Blake simply stared at him.

It had been a long, long time since Aidan had undressed Blake, and the circumstances had been very different then. He pulled Blake's T-shirt up from the hem. "Raise your arms."

Blake followed the instruction, and Aidan pulled the wet T-shirt off. Then he wrapped the towel around Blake's shoulders. Blake didn't move to do anything, so Aidan rubbed his upper body, then left the towel hanging around Blake's neck. He carefully tugged down Blake's swimsuit until it fell to the tile floor.

Blake's dick had retreated into his bush of pubic hair. Six inches, cut, Aidan remember Liam saying. Sure didn't look that big now, but Aidan had very clear memories of it when it was more lively.

That was all in the past, though. He pulled the towel off Blake's shoulders and handed it to him. "Don't make me do this, Blake."

Blake took the towel from Aidan and dried his groin, and then his legs. Aidan handed him the bikini briefs, which Blake stepped into. Then the slacks, the shirt, the socks and the shoes. Aidan finger-combed Blake's hair and turned him to the mirror. "That's the Blake Chennault I know. The attorney who fights like a tiger for what he wants. Now go out there and defend your husband."

Blake looked from the mirror to Aidan. "Thank you." Then he walked out, leaving Aidan to pick up the wet clothes and towel and stuff them into the suitcase.

Just like always, Aidan thought.

By the time he returned to the emergency room, Liam was waiting by the desk, but Blake had disappeared. "Ricardo's out of surgery, so Blake went to see him," Liam said.

In the background, an elderly woman wept quietly. A younger woman in shoulder-length dreadlocks and a floral minidress hugged her and said, "Don't worry, mama, doctor soon come."

Across from them sat a young father with coffee-colored skin and a haircut that made it look like a bush was growing out of his head. He cradled his right leg, wrapped in a clumsy blood-stained bandage. Aidan felt guilty that a white man, a visitor, had taken precedence over these locals, and hoped it was merely a matter of triage rather than privilege.

"How is your arm?" Aidan asked Liam. Tiny spots of red had bled through the white terrycloth.

"It's fine."

"You should have someone look at it while we're here," Aidan said. "You don't need to get an infection. We're going to be on planes for the next couple of days, so you can't decide to see a doctor when we're thirty thousand feet in the air."

Liam looked grim. "I want to make sure Ricardo is all right first."

"One has nothing to do with the other." Aidan grabbed Liam's good arm and coaxed him to his feet, then guided him over to the nurse at the desk, a jolly-looking heavyset woman in a pink uniform. "My husband cut his arm while rescuing Mr. Levy," he said to her. "Can you put him on your list?"

She stood up. "Let me see the wound."

Reluctantly, Liam unwound the white towel.

"That is a bad cut," she said. "When was the last time you had a tetanus shot?"

Liam looked at Aidan, who had both their passports in the front pocket of his cargo pants. He checked Liam's immunization card. "He had the Tdap vaccine eight years ago."

"The recommended interval is no longer than ten years between immunizations," the nurse said. "We'll let the doctor decide if he needs a booster shot. Please sit down and we will have someone see you as soon as possible."

The air conditioned hummed in the background. The boy with the cut leg was taken into the back, and a pair of young American women arrived, looking pale and dehydrated.

Detective Pickett appeared a few minutes later. "I did not expect to see you again," he said, as if it was their fault that Ricardo had been shot and they'd ended up in the emergency room.

Which Aidan figured it was, in a way. If they had been more careful in the choices they made, Ricardo might never have been a good target for the shooter.

Liam went on the offensive immediately. "Have you arrested the man who shot Mr. Levy?"

"We are pursuing our investigation. Please explain to me what happened."

Liam explained about getting into the inner tubes and floating down the lazy river. He, too, had seen Ricardo's body bounce against the back of the tube before he heard the shots.

"How many shots?"

Liam thought. "Three. I can't say for certain but I believe one of them hit Mr. Levy, another punctured the float, and the third went wild."

"That fits with our examination of the crime scene. We found one bullet on the floor of the river ride, and another embedded in the wall. We are continuing to examine the crime scene."

Aidan was relieved that Pickett no longer considered them adversaries. "Aren't guns outlawed here in the Bahamas?" he asked.

"For the most part, yes." Pickett frowned. "There are always exceptions to the rule. For example, you can legally have a gun on your boat when you dock at one of our marinas. You are prohibited from carrying it onshore. However, many people find ways around that."

"Does that mean our shooter got here by boat?" Liam asked.

Pickett shook his head. "We are not making any assumptions, though we are investigating all possibilities."

Pickett's cell phone rang then, the tone a lively mix of steel drums that reminded Aidan of the sound of the baggage claim area at the airport. Pickett turned away from them so they could not hear what he was saying.

When he ended the call, he turned back to them. "I must go. You will remain at the hotel?"

"We had reservations on a flight this evening to Philadelphia," Aidan said. "It doesn't look like we'll be able to make that, so assuming the hotel can accommodate us, we will stay there another night."

"One of your party was injured on their premises. They will bend over to keep you from suing them." He wagged a finger at them. You may not leave the Bahamas until I approve," Pickett said. "If you decide to change hotels, you must notify my office immediately."

Then he turned on his heel and left, dialing his cell phone as he walked. Aidan felt strange as he watched the man leave, almost as if he was still as vulnerable as he'd been in his bathing suit and T-shirt when the shooter attacked.

25 – Repercussions

"They're taking Ricardo up to the operating room now. There's a waiting room on the second floor."

Aidan turned to see Blake. Though he still looked upset, the old Blake Chennault was there in his stiff posture.

Blake's voice cracked. "He's lost a lot of blood, and the doctors aren't sure where the bleeding is coming from. They won't know until they open him up."

"I did some checking online. This is the best hospital in the Bahamas," Aidan said. "I'm sure they can handle a bullet wound. And knowing you're here to look after him, they won't dare make any mistakes."

Blake looked like a child who'd had his favorite lollipop taken away. "I hope you're right."

"I'll go with you," Aidan said. "I'll sit with you while you wait for the doctors to finish. Liam, you stay here until you get that arm seen to."

Blake's eyes opened wide. "What's wrong with Liam's arm?"

"It's nothing," Liam said.

"You still need to get it cleaned up and bandaged. No arguments, Billy boy."

Liam, whose legal first name was William, had been known as Billy from the time he was born, to distinguish him from his father, Big Bill. Upon his discharge from the SEALs he had chosen to be called Liam, and the only people who still called him Billy were his former teammates and his mother and sisters. His mother, not one of Aidan's favorite people, called him Billy boy when she wasn't happy with him.

"Bossy," Liam muttered, but he sat back down across from the old woman and her daughter.

Aidan took Blake's arm and led him to the elevator. Once they were settled on slightly more comfortable padded chairs, Blake said, "I want you to know, I don't blame you and Liam for what happened. Ricardo wanted to go on that river ride, and he and I both thought the threat was behind us."

"I'm glad you feel that way. Liam and I believe we have to let the clients call the final shots—no pun intended. All we can do is recommend. Liam was reluctant, but I admit I agreed with you. I thought it would be safe."

"Who do you think did it?"

Aidan shook his head. "No idea. Though it must be someone with a personal grudge against Ricardo. Someone who will suffer now that the information is public."

"What if he comes back?" Blake began to shake. "I can't keep doing this, being this nurturing, caring guy. These last few months have knocked me down." He looked at Aidan. "You know me better than anyone besides Ricardo. This is not the way I'm built. I'm too selfish."

Aidan resisted the urge to put his arm around Blake again. "You've been doing fine so far. Looking after Ricardo, making sure he takes his pills, going along with what he wants."

"But that's not us. We argue. We're both stubborn and we fight over every decision."

Aidan looked around the waiting room. It was painted a pale green, and the chairs were clustered in small groups, probably to give those waiting a sense of privacy. There was no one else in the room; not surprising, because it was a Friday afternoon.

"That's not the healthiest way to live, Blake. Maybe this situation is a wake-up call that if you love each other, you need to find a way to get along better."

"You're a relationship therapist now?"

There was a single painting on each wall, a beach scene probably done by a local artist. Aidan took some strength from the placid water around him and shook his head. "Nope. But I lived with you, and I know how I behaved when we were together. I let you make all the decisions, and sometimes I felt I was lost in that relationship."

Blake started to argue, but Aidan held up his hand. "Let me finish. A lot of that was my fault, and I made a conscious decision to change when I met Liam. You may have noticed, he's a strong, take-charge kind of guy."

Blake nodded. "He is indeed."

"And I yield to him a lot. Particularly when it comes to protecting clients. But I also stand up for myself more than I did when I was with you. We argue, sure, but we don't fight, and we both listen to each other. Liam gives in to me when he recognizes I'm right, and sometimes so that there's a balance between us."

Blake crossed his arms over his chest. "I don't know if I can do that. I'm so stubborn and set in my ways."

"And yet you forced yourself to change when Ricardo got sick. So you can do that. You don't have to make such a dramatic change, though. Just listen to him when talks."

"I do listen to him!" Blake protested. Immediately, though, he subsided. "I guess you're right. I don't listen enough. A lot of the time when we argue, we both realize that we were so caught up in the fight that we have lost track of what we cared about."

"You care about each other," Aidan said. "I see that in the way you look at each other. The way you've worried about him so much. Ricardo demonstrated a lot of courage when he insisted on giving his speech despite all the threats. You can have that kind of courage too."

Blake settled back into the armchair. They sat in silence for a while, until the door at the end of the room opened and a surgeon stepped out. He had toffee-colored skin that contrasted blindingly with the white of his scrubs. As he peeled off his rubber gloves he said, "Here with Mr. Levy?"

Blake stood. "Blake Chennault. Ricardo is my husband. How is he?"

"He'll be fine, after some rest. The bullet did not do much damage, so I only had to repair a couple of blood vessels. I understand the police are involved?"

Blake nodded.

"We gave him a powerful anesthetic so we could operate. He'll be knocked out for a couple of hours. I want to keep him overnight. Do you have plans to return home?"

"We had a flight this evening," Blake said. "Will he be able to travel tomorrow?"

"We'll have to see how he recovers. How long is your flight?

"About three hours, non-stop."

The doctor nodded. "When you add the travel time to the airport, and the wait there, plus whatever it takes to get to your home -- it could be as long as five hours, no?"

Blake nodded.

"He might be able to leave the hospital tomorrow, but I don't want him to be in transit for so long right away. Let's see how he recovers from the surgery, but perhaps you might plan to leave on Sunday."

Blake thanked him. "When can I see him?"

"The nurses will try to wake him for dinner around six o'clock, and you might be able to speak briefly with him before he goes back to sleep."

Aidan texted Liam, who was almost finished in the ER, and they met him downstairs. There was a white gauze bandage on Liam's lower arm, but nothing more, and the endorphins of relief swept through Aidan. "The doctor suggested we come back around six to see Ricardo. Why don't we get something to eat while we wait?"

"I'll stay here," Blake said.

"Stay here and brood," Aidan said. "Nope, you're coming with us."

"What if this guy comes after Ricardo again?"

"I'm going to call Pickett and see if he has arrested anyone yet," Liam said. "I'll ask him to station an officer outside Ricardo's room if there's still some danger."

Liam pulled Pickett's card from his wallet and dialed the number on it. He introduced himself and asked if the police had found the gunman yet. Then he turned aside to listen.

Aidan hated that habit of Liam's. He remembered the first day they met, back in Tunis, when Liam had turned away so that Aidan could not hear his phone call. Back then, it made sense. They didn't know each other, had no reason to trust one another.

Now, though, it was foolish. Why not let him and Blake hear the conversation? Liam was going to have to repeat it to them. But then he reminded himself of the conversation he'd had with Blake earlier. Some things about a husband you had to accept you were never going to change.

Surprisingly, Liam turned around as he was finishing the conversation. "I can't say that's good news, but at least it means Mr. Levy is safe. Thank you for sharing the information with me."

He ended the call. "The police arrested an Iranian national fleeing the hotel property, carrying a gun that matches the type used to shoot Ricardo."

Before Blake could interrupt, he said, "They won't have a ballistics match until next week, but it doesn't matter. The man confessed to sending the threatening emails to Ricardo, and to shooting him."

"Bastard," Blake said. "I hope they hang him. Do they have the death penalty in the Bahamas?"

"Doesn't matter. He has a diplomatic passport from Iran, and the Bahamian government doesn't want to risk an international incident. The man is being transported to the airport now."

"So we get nothing?" Blake demanded. "I want that man's balls for earrings!"

Aidan suppressed a snicker at the thought of Blake wearing earrings of any kind. "We get the satisfaction that Ricardo is out of danger." He put a hand on Blake's sleeve. "That has to be enough."

Blake stood there shaking, until he mastered himself and said, "I guess that's true."

They ate at a Chinese restaurant near the hospital, surrounded by Bahamians, many of them in hospital or hotel uniforms. They walked back to the hospital at six and Aidan and Liam saw Ricardo briefly, then left Blake with him for a few extra minutes.

When they got back to the hotel Liam texted Ryan Wood to let him and Ashley know what had happened, and the Woods, who weren't leaving until Sunday, promised to visit Ricardo the next morning.

Saturday morning Liam rose early, did his exercises and then left for the pool, while Aidan luxuriated in a nap in the comfortable hotel bed. They'd be traveling soon, back to Philadelphia and then to Nice, and he wanted to get his rest while he could.

Blake wouldn't let him sleep in too long, though. He was eager to get to the hospital and see Ricardo, and as soon as Liam returned from the pool, showered and dressed, they were in a cab to Nassau.

Ricardo was sitting up in bed when they got there, his dark curls wild but his color restored. Aidan was touched by the way Blake immediately went to him, kissed him, then finger-combed his hair.

Ryan and Ashley stopped by a short while later on their way to the straw market to pick up souvenirs. Ryan pulled Aidan and Liam aside. "Thought you might want to see this," he said, holding out his phone.

They read a CNN report that the negotiating team for the Iranian nuclear deal had announced to the press that there were new developments in the negotiations, which had been suspended. "Looks like Ricardo is getting his wish," Ryan said. "His story is causing repercussions internationally."

"Not surprising, if the man who shot him was an Iranian official," Aidan said.

Blake insisted that Aidan and Liam go shopping with Ryan and Ashley, while he stayed with Ricardo. Ashley wanted to buy knickknacks for her colleagues and a gift for the woman who was watching their dog.

The market was lively, a high-ceiling building crowded with stalls and tables. Reggae music echoed against the tin roof, competing with the calls of the vendors. Straw had been configured into every kind of product imaginable, from baskets to hats to dolls with yarn faces. Misshapen mugs that read "I got smashed in the Bahamas" competed for table space with pink conch shells the size of Aidan's head.

Aidan noticed that Liam no longer swiveled his head regularly, surveying the crowd for threats. He laughed when Ryan mugged with a colorful scarf, pulling it over his head like a Navy Mata Hari.

Aidan was relieved to be away from Blake and Ricardo. Even when they were quiet, there was a tension between them that shimmered in the air. He checked his watch and counted the hours until they would return the clients to Philadelphia, and he and Liam could head back to their own lives.

Aidan found a squeaky alligator toy to bring home for Hayam. The little dog had surely missed her daddies, though Aidan was sure Slava and Thierry had spoiled her in their absence.

They bought cold cans of pineapple-flavored Goombay Punch soda and fresh-fried conch fritters. Ricardo said you used to be a teacher," Ashley said, as they walked under the high tin roof.

"I have a degree in TESOL," Aidan said. "For the most part, I stopped teaching when I met Liam and started working with him, though I did teach in an English immersion program in Tunisia while we were assigned to protect a student there."

"Do you miss it?"

Aidan remembered the conversation with Liam that had triggered their journey, when Liam admitted that he missed the excitement of close protection work.

Aidan shrugged. "Sure. But I do some teaching now as part of the company we run, instructing employees about personal and cyber security. It's not the same as establishing that one-on-one connection with students, seeing them get more confident with language."

"My college has a mentoring initiative going on now," Ashley said. "We're encouraged to do a lot of one-on-one meetings, encourage them in their studies and so on. Honestly, it's pretty exhausting. They all want to know what kind of jobs they can get, rather than developing critical thinking and writing skills."

"What department are you in?"

"It's called Near Eastern and Judaic Studies, and we mix history, culture and religion. Lots of Jewish students, obviously, trying to connect to their heritage. But we also have a lot of kids who want to work in global politics, or the oil industry."

As they talked, Aidan experienced a pang of regret that he'd never been able to follow that path, securing a full-time teaching job, but by the time Ashely finished explaining how bad her students' writing was, he was back to being glad that he'd joined Liam in close protection.

They stopped to watch a smooth-skinned old man chisel a piece of wood until the fin of a dolphin emerged. We were all a work in progress, Aidan thought.

"I'm impressed at how well you and Liam work together," Ashley said, as they circled back toward the market entrance. "Ryan and I tend to fight more than my parents think is appropriate. They want me to be a good Jewish wife, a proper Latina, and defer everything to him, but I'm just not made that way."

"I learned a lot from my time with Blake," Aidan said. "As you've probably seen, he's very bossy and wants his own way. I used to defer everything to him and eventually I realized that our relationship was very one-sided. It was all Blake, all the time, and though I didn't know it at the time, it was suffocating me."

He smiled at her. "You and Ryan seem to have a good balance. That's very rare."

"I love him more than anything, and I know he feels the same way about me," Ashley said. "And that's what keeps us going."

"Us, too," Aidan said. He squeezed her hand.

As they were about to leave the market, Blake texted that Ricardo was ready to leave the hospital, and Aidan and Liam said goodbye to the Woods. "We ought to keep in touch," Ashley said. "I'm hoping to get a travel grant to Europe next year to research the migration of Sephardic and Mizrahi Jews from North Africa to Spain, Portugal and France."

Aidan kissed her cheek and promised that if the Woods came to the Riviera, they were welcome in Banneret-les-Vaux. "I'd love to help you out with your research, too."

Liam had already hailed a cab by then, so Aidan kissed Ashley's cheek again, shook Ryan's hand, then jumped into the cab. As usual, the streets were crowded with jitneys, trucks and taxis. They swerved around a horse-drawn carriage making its way slowly down Bay Street.

Ricardo and Blake were already waiting in the hotel lobby, and Aidan jumped out to help Ricardo into the front seat of the cab. Blake joined them in the rear, with Aidan squeezed into the middle.

Aidan noticed that Ricardo had laid his head back and appeared to doze. "What did the doctor say?" Aidan asked Blake. "When will Ricardo be well enough to travel?"

"I booked us flights tomorrow afternoon," Blake said. "The sooner we get out of this country, the happier I'll be. I've already scheduled Ricardo for a follow up visit with our internist in Philly on Monday afternoon."

Blake helped Ricardo out of the front seat when they pulled up at the hotel, and threaded his arm in his husband's as they walked into the lobby. "I think we'll order room service," Blake said, when they reached the elevator. "Why don't you guys go out to dinner and relax? Ricardo and I both appreciate everything you've done for us."

After seeing the clients safely up to the suite, Aidan and Liam went to an Italian restaurant in one of the hotel towers. It was an elegant dining room with Doric columns supporting a frescoed ceiling. They sat in the middle of the room, not caring who was around them.

Liam surprised Aidan when the server came by, saying, "My husband and I will both have glasses of the pinot grigio."

When the wine arrived, Liam lifted his glass to Aidan in a toast. "To another assignment completed." When their glasses clinked, a couple of drops spilled onto the tablecloth.

"Call that the angels' share," Aidan said. "And thank our guardian angels that we're going home safely, and as always, that we're together."

Dedication

To Marc: You might think I'm crazy, but all I want is you.

About the Author

A native of Bucks County, PA, Neil is a graduate of the University of Pennsylvania, Columbia University and Florida International University, where he received his MFA in creative writing. He lives in South Florida with his husband and two rambunctious golden retrievers. He is a four-time finalist for the Lambda Literary Award in Best Gay Mystery and Best Gay Romance.

A professor of English at Broward College's South Campus, he has written and edited many other books; details can be found at his website, **http://www.mahubooks.com**. He is also past president of the Florida chapter of Mystery Writers of America.

www.ingramcontent.com/pod-product-compliance
Lightning Source LLC
LaVergne TN
LVHW012014060526
838201LV00061B/4310